LOVERS NEVER LIE

Stacia Roberts has always played it safe, yet, longing for adventure, she travels to Greece expecting sunshine and excitement — and gets more than she'd ever bargained for. When strangers try to kill her, she suspects her fellow traveller Andrew Moore might be the enemy — but is he really a friend? Andrew blames himself for his wife's death. Then he falls in love with Stacia, vowing to keep her safe, a difficult task when he discovers she's an international thief.

GAEL MORRISON

LOVERS
NEVER LIE

Complete and Unabridged

LINFORD
Leicester

First published in the
United States of America in 2002

First Linford Edition
published 2013

British Library CIP Data

Morrison, Gael.
    Lovers never lie. - -
    (Linford romance library)
    1. Romantic suspense novels.
    2. Large type books.
    I. Title II. Series
    813.6–dc23

    ISBN 978–1–4448–1431–6

Published by
F. A. Thorpe (Publishing)
Anstey, Leicestershire

Set by Words & Graphics Ltd.
Anstey, Leicestershire
Printed and bound in Great Britain by
T. J. International Ltd., Padstow, Cornwall

This book is printed on acid-free paper

To my husband Ron
and to our sons,
Allen, Andrew, Peter and Alex
with love and heartfelt gratitude

1

Damn! Where had *she* come from?

Andrew Moore snatched up his *Cubs* cap from the front seat of his car, settled it on his head and yanked it low over his eyes. A woman like *that* couldn't be involved in this. She was no more than a girl, for God's sake.

A gust of wind caught the woman's skirt as she paused at the foot of the steps, blowing it up around her thighs, the material a blue mist against the tan of her skin. She was all legs. A woman's legs, not a girl's.

Her hands swept down and forced her skirt tight against her body. Nice curves, though a little thin. Andrew sank deeper into his seat.

'Get a move on, lady,' he muttered. 'Collect your damn charity money, or whatever the hell it is you're doing here, and go.'

Nobody would make the pick up with her standing on the front steps. And if they did, she'd get caught in the middle. Might even get hurt, as Nancy had.

A too familiar sense of helplessness and rage washed over him at the thought of his wife. Resolutely, Andrew shut his mind on his memories.

The woman looked cold out in that breeze. Fooled by the sunny weather? Or simply an optimist? The way she clutched her sweater around her breasts . . . Fool! Don't look at her breasts! He had more important things to worry about than some under-dressed female out to catch a cold.

Andrew forced his gaze from the woman and watched a cat instead, as it streaked from bush to bush in the yard of a neighboring house. But when the cat slipped beneath a porch and disappeared, he slowly, reluctantly glanced back toward the steps. The woman was still there.

She lifted her hand, reached to press

the buzzer. The wind riffled her straight brown hair and for an instant exposed the skin at the base of her neck. He could almost feel the shiver streak across her shoulders then shimmy down the rest of her body.

She pulled her sweater tighter and turned to look around. Her eyes — a dark brown — although why he was convinced of that from this distance he didn't know — met his, then swiftly snapped away again.

Her chest rose, then fell, and for a second time she rang the buzzer. This time the door opened so suddenly, someone must have been standing and waiting on the other side. The woman stepped inside, the door slammed shut, and she was gone.

Andrew glowered at the small clock on the dashboard of his car ticking away the minutes while he sat and waited. He rolled his shoulders to ease his bunched, tight muscles. A lone sheet of newspaper fluttered along the surface of the grass and slammed against the steps where the woman had stood.

No sign of her coming out again. Andrew's jaw tensed. Watching her enter the house had been like watching a butterfly flutter into a spider's web. He didn't know what she was there for, but if she wasn't out in five minutes, he was going in after her.

★ ★ ★

Stacia Roberts hid her distaste as the dry, bony fingers of the man touched hers. The whole house felt dry, as desiccated as a body in a tomb. And it was hot, like a furnace compared to the chill outside. She could scarcely bear to follow the man into his study, where the heat, combined with the musty odor of ancient, overstuffed furniture and seldom dusted bookshelves, was stifling.

The man slipped behind the massive oak desk dominating the room. 'Have a seat, Miss Roberts.' He gestured towards the cracked leather chair in front of the desk.

Stacia lowered herself carefully, as the seams on the chair looked as though they might rip apart at the slightest touch.

'So glad, Miss Roberts, that you answered my advertisement.' The man surveyed her from head to foot. 'You look quite perfect for the job.'

'Thank-you, Mr., uh . . .'

He hesitated for an instant. 'Stone,' he finally said.

'Mr. Stone,' Stacia echoed. 'I didn't realize there were any special requirements for the job.'

'No, no, nothing of the sort,' he replied. 'I meant you look . . . reliable.'

She was reliable, all right. But not for much longer. Footloose and fancy free. That's what she wanted. No obligations, no complications . . . no money.

Stacia sighed. Reliable meant getting this job and, with it, a ticket to Greece. She smothered another sigh. She could do reliable for a while longer.

'How big is the package you want me to take?' she asked.

He reached into the bottom drawer of his desk and pulled out a brown paper package. He pushed aside a framed picture of a younger, thinner, more fully-haired version of himself and a dark-haired woman standing before an old stone church and passed the package to Stacia.

Whatever was inside was soft. Clothing? Stacia wondered. She placed the package back on the desk and glanced at Mr. Stone, surprised.

'There's a sweater in there,' he explained. 'Mrs. Andropolous knit it for her husband's daughter-in-law.'

'Her *husband's* daughter-in-law?'

'She's my client's second wife.' He leaned towards her, spittle flecking the corner of his mouth.

Stacia drew back, the chair's leather giving way obligingly.

'Wrapped in the sweater is Mr. Andropolous's last will and testament,' Stone continued solemnly, 'to be delivered only into the hands of his eldest son, Darius. Mr. Andropolous's younger son is not happy about the new will. My client is afraid he'll attempt to intercept it.' Mr. Stone stared sternly at Stacia. 'You mustn't let on to anyone that you have the parcel with you.'

Stacia frowned. 'Wouldn't it be safer just to mail it or file it in your office?'

'Of course it would.' He suddenly straightened, his movement bringing a protesting squeal from the wheels of his chair. 'But there's no telling Mr. Andropolous that. The old man doesn't trust *any* public institutions — banks, the postal service — let alone a lawyer's office.'

Stacia nodded. Grandfather Roberts had been the same. They had found stashes of money everywhere after he died, under his mattress, in a paint can in the garage, tacked to the back of a picture frame. His attorney had shaken his head in despair.

Grandfather Roberts had also insisted on hanging on to his own will. It had been days before they finally located it wrapped in plastic and tucked between two pot roasts in the freezer.

Mr. Stone placed an envelope on top of the package, and released it from his fingers slowly. 'I think you'll find everything you need in here. Airline tickets, money, hotel reservations for your first few nights in Athens.' His brow creased. 'Mr. Andropolous's son is a very busy man, is often out of Greece on business. He intends to meet you at the hotel upon your arrival, but he may well be delayed.'

'Don't worry, Mr. Stone.' Stacia took the envelope and tucked it into her purse. Then she picked up the package. 'I'll bring this to him safely.' There, that had been said with more certainty than she actually felt.

The idea of foreign travel both attracted and terrified her. All the more reason to do it. *Safe* was not something she wanted anymore. She'd been safe too long.

Stacia stood and followed Stone back down the dusty hall, shook his brittle fingers one last time, then stepped out into the crisp spring morning.

The grey car was still parked two doors down. The driver must be asleep, he was sitting so still, his chin tucked into his chest and his hat pulled over his eyes. Strange place to sleep.

He had startled her earlier — staring at her like that. She had, of course, not looked at him properly. Dangerous to do that in the city, her father had always said. Avert your gaze. Don't talk to strangers.

Stacia brushed away the moisture that had welled in her eyes. She'd always been impatient with her father's advice, had ignored it for the most part, but now he was gone, she missed it.

She straightened her shoulders and started down the steps. Her father might be right about Chicago, but in Greece she planned to indulge her natural inclination to look people in the eye. She intended to meet all sorts, talk to anyone she cared to. Excitement surged through her, and she quickly walked away.

* * *

No matter which way she juggled her suitcases, Stacia's arms felt as though they might snap in two. She had considered investing in a suitcase on wheels instead of making do with Grandmother Roberts' heavy old case, but every dollar saved would lengthen her stay in Greece.

With a sigh, she squeezed her carry-on case more tightly against her body, until suddenly it slipped from beneath her arm. She lunged for it and the suitcase in her other hand clattered to the floor. It sprang open, the old metal latches not up to the strain.

Cotton dresses, shorts and tops, lingerie and bathing suits cascaded forth in a kaleidoscope of purple, pink and turquoise, ending in a jumbled heap on the floor.

Her new silk panties slid across the linoleum and stopped against solid brown shoe leather.

A man's shoe.

Heat swept Stacia's cheeks. Without looking up, she leaned over the precariously tilted suitcase and snatched up her underwear.

'Let me help you,' a voice offered.

'No, thank you,' Stacia said. She reached for the clothes nearest her and jumbled them helter-skelter back into her case. She had spent a long time packing, had folded each item just so. The travel guide she'd read had promised that judicious packing and the right blend of synthetics would assure a wrinkle-free arrival. All that mattered now was to rescue her personal belongings from the gaze of a stranger.

She stretched toward a particularly elusive bikini top, but pulled back again when she encountered a hand, a man's hand. A warm current shot up her arm and through to her chest, leaving a peculiar tingling in its wake. She glanced upward and found herself staring into the face of the man belonging to the shoe.

No sign of laughter was evident on

his lips, but it lurked in his eyes — impossibly blue eyes, the same blue as his sweater. He picked up her bikini top and, dangling it from between two fingers, offered it to her.

'Thank you,' she said, taking care not to touch him again as she took it from him. She'd been thrown by the odd sensation when their fingers met the first time.

Now his amusement spread to his lips, lips made for laughter, full and mobile.

'I can manage the rest,' she said firmly, pulling her gaze from his lips. The flush warming her cheeks now spread to her neck.

He ignored her and with one broad sweep of his arm scooped up the rest of her clothes. He pulled the suitcase toward him, Stone's parcel scraping the floor beneath it.

'Stop!' Stacia cried, reaching for the package. 'You'll tear it!'

The man was faster. He released her clothes and knelt before her, then lifted the suitcase and snatched up the parcel.

'Looks important,' he said. The sapphire blue of his eyes darkened to the ebony of a night sky.

He looked as fierce as the Greek warrior, Ulysses, Stacia thought dazedly, with his high cheekbones and deep set eyes. Intelligent and perceptive, they matched the man's face.

She shook her head, tried to escape from the spell he cast over her. This wasn't one of her library books, and this man was no Greek God. This man had Mr. Andropolous's property and was busy pressing and probing the package as a child might do a Christmas present.

'Well?' he asked, glancing up from the package. He stared across at her. One eyebrow shot up and disappeared behind the shock of black hair covering his forehead.

'It's nothing important,' Stacia said tensely, holding her hand out for the parcel.

'Clothes?' he asked. His fingers sank into the brown paper, fell just short of ripping it.

'Do you always pry into other people's belongings?' Stacia demanded.

'I'm not usually gathering up a beautiful woman's intimate apparel from an airport floor,' he replied with a smile. But his body seemed rigid — rock hard where it should be relaxed. He didn't release his hold on the package.

Beautiful? Stacia frowned. What did this man want?

'No *gentleman* would pick up a woman's personal belongings,' she said crossly, 'then have the bad manners to comment on them.'

His smile widened to a grin. 'No one's ever accused me of being a gentleman before, and you haven't answered my question.'

'It's a sweater, if you must know.' She didn't like the way he watched her. 'Nothing exciting.'

She wasn't cut out for this kind of work, didn't know how to lie. Didn't *want* to know how to lie. Yet, here she was doing it.

Damn it, all she wanted was to have her parcel back. She thrust out her hand again.

The man ignored it and gave the parcel another squeeze. The wrapping paper crackled ominously, clearly strained by his examination.

Stacia cleared her throat. 'My parcel,' she said firmly.

In answer, the man set the suitcase upright, dumped clothes and parcel in together, then slammed the lid shut. He snapped the locks closed and took a firm grip on the handle.

'You need a new suitcase,' he said, standing, her bag still in his hand. 'This one looks as though it came across on the Mayflower.' He held out his hand as though to help her up.

Had she gone completely crazy? Was it his eyes compelling her to place her hand in his, or the implacable way he reached for her? Whatever the reason, however it happened, when his palm engulfed hers, it felt good. He pulled her up beside him, her body inches from his own, and she felt the zing of attraction, a connection beyond the physical.

Hastily, she snatched her hand away. She didn't want to feel connected to anyone again.

'Which gate are you going to?' the man asked.

'Why?'

His eyebrows rose. 'You look as though you could use some help.'

'I'll get a sky cap.'

His gaze swept the cavernous length of O'Hare airport and the hundreds of people charging to and fro; helpful bodies in blue conspicuously absent.

'Good luck,' he said, facing her once more. 'I'd be glad to help,' he added softly.

'I wouldn't want you to go to the trouble.' She reached for her suitcase.

'No trouble,' he said, evading her reach. He stepped away, carrying her suitcase as though it weighed nothing. With another easy movement, he picked up his own leather satchel.

Black hair curled around the nape of his neck. Wiry hair, and thick, like Samson's hair in the story of Delilah.

Mythical characters on her brain again! She had to forget about heroes and books. If she compared everyone she encountered with people she had read about in books, she would never experience life. Besides, when she got back from this trip, she didn't intend to be a librarian anymore. She would go to the university and study architecture as she had always wanted, perhaps live overseas. She would focus her attention on how buildings were made and try to restrain this passion for other people's stories.

'I can manage,' she insisted.

He raised one thick brow.

Her heart skipped a beat.

'Gate 47,' she murmured, pushing aside every warning her father had ever uttered about men and what they wanted and what they would do to get it. Meeting men was a good thing, in her opinion. She had been hoping to meet some on this trip. Good-looking men, with whom she could have fun.

'Right,' he said. He strode off without so much as a backward glance.

'Wait!' she called out, stunned by his quick departure.

He didn't even break stride.

Stacia sucked in an angry breath and gathered up her carry-on bag and purse. She went after him, but he walked too quickly. Even without her suitcase, it seemed impossible to catch him.

The airport was jammed. Businessmen mostly, who, intent on their route, stalked along oblivious to everyone else, and woe to anyone who got in their way.

The stranger was already far ahead. Luckily, he was tall or she'd never be able to see him over the crowd.

What if he took off with her bag? Stacia quickened her step. Perspiration trickled into her eyes. She couldn't see him anymore. She peered ahead anxiously, got one glimpse of his head as it bobbed into sight, then just as swiftly, was gone again.

Stacia swore under her breath and forced her feet faster. She hadn't seen him turn off, but if he hadn't, where was he? Her heart began to pound, and her throat burned. No air. Too much air. Had to slow down. Couldn't.

Oh God, where was he?

Gate 47.

At last. She stood stock still and shut her eyes tight. Maybe when she opened them, a miracle would occur and he'd be there.

'What on earth are you doing?'

Her eyelids snapped wide at the sound of his voice, and like magic the rest of him appeared in front of her.

'Meditating?' he asked mildly.

'Praying for divine intervention.'

'Did you think I'd made off with your bag?'

'You were going awfully fast.'

'Sorry,' he apologized softly, shrugging as he did so, the movement graceful and uniquely European.

Was he Greek? Mr. Andropolous's younger son might look like this man. Or perhaps he was some other faceless relative determined to get his hands on the old man's will. Uncertainty seeped through her like water through sand. Silently, she held out her hand for her suitcase.

The man simply stared at her. A frown creased his brow. 'Enjoy your trip,' he finally said, and handed over her bag.

There was no avoiding the touch of his fingers this time. They only rested against hers for the briefest of moments, but the sensation returned. It must be electricity, like the shock you got walking across carpets in an over-heated room.

Stacia's heart sank. It wasn't that kind of electricity at all.

2

First Class. With a contented sigh, Stacia settled into the wide, comfortable seat. Six months ago, she would never have imagined herself in First Class on an airplane bound for Greece.

Her father would have been against the idea. Too dangerous he would have said. Too foreign. Although he had said the same thing about Chicago, had nixed her plans to attend the university there, had even protested her infrequent shopping trips, saying the stores in their own small town had everything she needed.

And Grandmother Roberts . . . Whenever Stacia brought up the idea of traveling abroad, her grandmother's lips had tightened. No proper dinners to be had abroad, she said. No turkey and stuffing. No roast beef and mashed potatoes.

Stacia grinned. The only foreign food she had ever convinced her grandmother to try was lasagna. Even then the old woman had stared at it suspiciously, and sniffed it once or twice before raising a morsel to her lips. When she took her second bite, Stacia's father had winked at Stacia from his end of the table.

The open wound in Stacia's heart still gnawed at her chest. Her father had been dead for months, but the grieving didn't ease. She still missed him. As she did her mother.

She had only been twelve when her mother died, too young to understand the irrationality of the guilt that pierced her body-numbing grief. She had believed then it was *her* fault her mother had become sick, that if she had been a better daughter, hadn't argued so much, her mother wouldn't have got cancer. Wouldn't have died and left her and her father all alone.

She'd stood frozen by her mother's deathbed and had privately vowed to care for her father in her mother's place. She had managed it, too, had cleaned the house, made the meals, even worked in the local library instead of going on to the university.

It wasn't until her father died that Stacia realized how wrapped up she had been in his life, so worried about his happiness, she hadn't bothered with her own. And he had let her, for it kept her close and safe.

Stacia rolled her shoulders, released the tension gathering there. Her father was dead. No amount of grieving would bring him back. It was time now for adventure, perhaps even a little romance.

'Is it safe to sit here?'

She knew that voice.

'Or will your luggage fall on my head?'

'What are *you* doing here?' Stacia demanded, reluctantly twisting around to see him.

'Going on vacation,' the man with the sapphire eyes replied. He stretched up and slapped his satchel next to hers in the overhead compartment, then snapped the compartment door shut and flopped into the seat next to her. 'Seems I'm not the only one.' He faced her. 'Or are you going to Greece on business?'

'Vacation,' she said lightly. 'A bit of adventure.' She frowned. 'You didn't tell me you were on this flight?'

He settled his seat belt over his hips and fastened it, his elbow passing precariously close to her breast. She leaned as far away from him as possible.

'I didn't know we were on the same flight,' he replied. 'When I met you, I hadn't had a chance to look at my ticket yet. Didn't know which gate my flight took off from.' He shot her a swift grin. 'It seemed safer to get you where you needed to be first.'

'I don't need anyone to keep me safe.' She hated the very word. If there was any way to eliminate it from the dictionary, she would.

'It's not *your* safety I'm concerned with,' he replied, with a chuckle. 'It's the poor sucker unlucky enough to get in your way the next time you toss your luggage around.'

'I did not throw my — '

'You've brought too many things. The first rule of traveling on your own, Miss Roberts, is to travel light.' He smiled smugly. 'Like me.'

The heat drained from Stacia's face. 'How do you know my name?'

Before he could answer, the plane jolted into action. As it raced down the runway, Stacia grasped her arm rest. The aircraft shimmied and rattled, until at last it swept into the sky.

The man glanced sideways, his gaze probing her face the way his fingers had probed her package. 'It's on your suitcase,' he whispered solemnly.

Her breath escaped in a rush, and as it did, the plane straightened, found the correct elevation and leveled off. A fellow traveler. That's all he was. Stone's warning had made her paranoid.

Andrew studied the face of the girl beside him. If Stacia Roberts had nothing to hide, why had she turned so white? And why would she care if he knew her name?

Still . . . he shifted in his seat. She was difficult to figure, didn't seem the sort to be a player in this game. But if the past had taught him anything at all, it had taught him it was dangerous to make assumptions. Especially about women!

And if this woman suspected he was on to her, he'd never get what he wanted.

'What's *your* name?' she demanded, in a low husky voice. It shouldn't have matched her face with those clear brown eyes and upturned nose, but somehow it did, hinting at passion and depth.

Andrew gave himself a mental shake. It didn't matter how she looked or sounded.

Stacia Roberts was beginning to get to him and that had to stop.

'Did you hear me?' she asked, her face plainly anxious.

He opened his mouth, then closed it

again, suddenly undecided. If he gave his real name, she'd know he was on to her, yet if she reacted, he'd have his answer. Besides which, names were tricky, hard to conceal, especially with passports, traveler's cheques, and credit cards.

'Andrew Moore,' he replied finally, frowning as he saw the distrust in her eyes.

'Where are you from?' she asked.

'Here, there, and everywhere.' He shrugged, deliberately vague.

She stared at him with unwavering eyes.

No you don't, lady. He averted his gaze. He had too much at stake to be pulled into this woman's web with innocent looks.

'I mean *originally*,' she persisted.

He bit back an oath and faced her again. 'Small town south of Chicago.'

Her eyes darkened to the deep brown of the earth after a rain. A man could get lost in eyes like hers — could get wrapped in their promise and never escape. It was almost a relief when she turned and stared straight ahead.

'You look as though your family originally came from Italy.' She spoke as if she were reluctant to speak at all. 'Or . . . or Greece?' The last word all but disappeared in the hum of conversation around them.

Greek relatives. He thought quickly. Might be useful to admit to a few. Easier to follow her around the country if he could casually mention a cousin here, or an uncle there.

'My mother was Greek.' He repressed a grin. His mother would turn in her grave if she could hear him say such a thing. She'd been British to the bone, had never even lost her accent despite the years she lived with his father's midwest twang, and had carefully tutored them all on proper elocution, insisting fuzzy vowels were the quickest route to social disgrace.

'Oh,' Stacia Roberts said.

'Care for a drink before dinner, sir?' The polite cadence of the flight attendant's voice reassured Stacia and her breathing steadied as Andrew Moore transferred his penetrating gaze to the smiling woman in the aisle.

'Scotch, please,' he answered, without hesitation. 'And a glass of white wine for the lady.'

'No, thank you,' Stacia said sharply.

He turned to her. 'I could have sworn wine would be your drink. What would you like then?' His tone was formal, his voice studiously polite.

She could refuse to have anything, but her mouth was so dry. 'I'd like — ' She cast around for something wonderfully wild to order, something she had never tried before. ' — a bourbon and water, please.'

Her father's drink. Not a nice drink for a woman, her grandmother would have said, but what did she know, living in the past as she had?

At least she had managed to startle Andrew Moore. Incredible how satisfying that felt. He had the most expressive eyebrows she'd ever seen.

When he frowned they met in a bushy bridge above his nose. Wine indeed! She reached across him accepting her drink from the flight attendant.

No ice. Stacia stared at her glass doubtfully. Her father had never had ice. But her drink looked a little . . . brown, not thirst-quenching at all. She snuck a sideways peek at Andrew. He was watching her still. No time for second thoughts. Her father had liked bourbon. So would she.

She raised the drink to her lips slowly. Her stomach quailed as the fumes assailed her nose. Wine didn't smell.

But this was what traveling was all about. Trying new things. Off with the old, and on with the new. She should be grateful to Andrew Moore. She took a sip.

No, not grateful. The bourbon scorched a path down her throat into her stomach. Stacia twisted her head toward the window and pretended an interest in the blackness outside. She'd never be able to drink the entire glass. Damn it, there was no reason she had to.

'Drink all right?'

'Fine, thanks.' She faced him again, even attempted a smile. Difficult, with a mouth shrunken from the taste of bourbon.

He took a long sip of his scotch then set his glass on the table in front of him. His hands were nice. Long fingers, but strong and capable looking.

His face was the same. Fine, intelligent features, determined chin . . . Not a man you'd want to oppose. She turned away. No reason to imagine she would have to.

'Is this your first trip to Greece?'

Reluctantly, she faced him again. 'Yes,' she answered shortly. Her first trip *anywhere*.

'How long will you be staying?'

Was he simply being polite, one traveler to another? Surely there was nothing ominous about the question.

'I'm not sure.' Her answer startled

her, yet filled her with a sudden pleasure. It had sounded so uncertain, as though she hadn't any plans at all. In the past, she'd always known exactly where she was going and what she would be doing. And had hated it, she suddenly realized.

'I thought I'd play it by ear,' she added impulsively.

He frowned.

She felt a surge of power. She could do whatever she wanted with no one to answer to, could drift with the wind or fly with the birds.

'You'll want to be careful, you know — '

'Careful!'

'A woman traveling alone is a perfect target.'

'For what?'

His slow gaze seemed to take in every inch of her. A wave of heat began in the pit of her stomach and swept outward until it blazed her skin. She'd seen men look at other women like that, but never at *her*.

'For *that*,' he said forcibly. 'In the Mediterranean, the men will take one look at you, then pounce.'

'I can take care of myself.' She ignored the flames fanning her cheeks, and brought her glass to her lips. This time the bourbon went down more easily, but did nothing to quench the fire within.

'I wouldn't count on it,' Moore replied, too fast, too smooth.

Anger boiled up, overwhelming that other heat he had aroused. 'Look Mr. . . . *Moore*, I don't need you to tell me what to watch out for.' She sucked in a shaky breath. 'The most dangerous man I'm likely to meet in Greece is *you*!'

'You might be right, Miss Roberts.' His eyes grew distant. 'You might be right.'

★   ★   ★

Stacia scrunched her eyes more tightly shut, but she couldn't avoid the light hitting her squarely in the face. Morning. She must have slept after all. A weight pressed against her, a warm weight

33

. . . nice. The smooth-rough texture of skin brushed her hand. Someone else's skin.

She snapped her eyes open. Andrew Moore was leaning across her, his face just inches from her own.

'What are you doing?' she demanded, her body stiffening. His eyes weren't simply blue. There was grey in them, also, and they shifted and changed with the light, from slate to almost black.

He smiled at her, a casual, sexy sort of grin. But she couldn't smile back. Not with his lips this close, lips she suddenly felt like kissing.

His gaze flickered to her mouth, and the black in his eyes suddenly dominated.

'Just fastening your seat belt,' he explained. 'I didn't want to wake you.'

'I can do it myself.' She lifted his hand away from her side. His skin was warm. And smooth. Though a roughness was there, also, as though he knew about hard work. An exhilarating hand to hold. With a sharp intake of breath, she dropped it.

He pulled away from her slowly. The disappearance of his warmth left her strangely bereft. But she was able to breathe again now that he no longer touched her. She searched for the end of her seat belt buried somewhere between them, and clicked it shut.

The plane dipped.

'We're almost there,' Andrew murmured.

Stacia ran her hand through her hair. She must look a mess. Andrew had not only combed his hair, but had shaved and put on aftershave. The scent of it tickled her nose and sent a tingle spiralling through her chest. She swallowed hard, and turned to the window. When she released the blind, the yellow warmth shafting through transformed into a blanket. Through the glass, she could see the aircraft already making its approach to the runway.

'Where are you staying in Athens?' Andrew asked.

'With . . . with friends.' Frowning, Stacia reached beneath her seat and brought her purse to her lap. She unclasped it and slipped her fingers inside.

The envelope containing her hotel reservations and money was still tucked between her passport and wallet. The paper crackled as her fingers closed around it.

She wanted to believe he had asked the question from mere politeness, as one traveler to another, but she'd been unable to shake the nagging suspicion of the night before, that Andrew Moore could be Andropolous's younger son.

'Let's get together for a drink in Athens,' he suggested.

Startled, Stacia released the envelope back into her purse. 'Perhaps,' she said evasively.

'If you give me your friend's phone number — '

'The number is in my suitcase. When we get off the plane maybe I can dig it out.'

He frowned. 'What about the rest of your trip? Does your travel agent have you well organized?'

'As much as I need to be.' Hotel

reservations, tickets, and a thick wad of Greek drachmas were in that envelope, but they weren't from any travel agent, and they weren't for Andrew to see.

The plane rocked as it hit the runway. Stacia dropped her purse onto her lap and took hold of the arm rests.

'It's all right,' Andrew said softly, seeming to know she feared the landing. He covered her hand with his.

She pulled her hand away.

'Travel rule number two,' he added. 'Never let *anyone* see you're afraid.'

'Who's afraid,' she said fiercely, forcing herself to loosen her grip.

'Present company excluded, of course.'

'I don't intend to trust anyone.'

'Good,' he said.

Unexpectedly, his approval warmed her.

When the plane rolled to a stop, he snapped open his seat belt. Standing, he pulled down both their bags from the overhead compartment.

Stacia stood, also, her legs stiff from disuse. She took her bag from Andrew's outstretched hand and stepped into the aisle before him.

Goodbye, she had intended to say upon landing, and have a good trip. But suddenly, now that the moment had come, she wished they were still in the air.

Passengers surged behind them, jamming Andrew up against her. His body was hard beneath his loose-fitting clothes, and incredibly warm. She fit against him perfectly, the top of her head coming just beneath his chin.

Comfortable. She shifted her body forward. Comfortable was not what she wanted; independence was what she craved.

The passengers shuffled forward like prisoners in a chain gang. Stacia returned the flight attendant's parting smile, un-clenched her stiff fingers and stepped off the plane.

It was warmer than Chicago. Perhaps the air-conditioning was off in the termi-nal building. She glanced around. There might not be any air-conditioning.

The signs on the wall were indecipherable. Different alphabet, different sounds. No hope of figuring it out. But the uncertainty was exciting, even if a little unnerving. Better not let Andrew see she was nervous. He had an irritating tendency to want to help.

She would follow the crowd. They seemed to know where they were going. There! Something in English. Money changer. Might have guessed.

Andrew's aftershave still assailed her senses. Stacia tried to breathe more shallowly. She stared past the barriers to the waiting crowds, and her excitement grew.

This place was nothing like home. The people themselves didn't look much different, although their clothes were distinctively Greek, with the black shawls around the old women's shoulders and the fisherman caps on the grizzled grey heads of the men. It was more an atmosphere, an ambiance, an air of promise.

'Need any money changed?' Andrew asked, his breath warm against her ear.

'No thanks.' The envelope in her purse held plenty of money, both Greek and American.

The line suddenly moved faster. The luggage carousel was just ahead, with her suitcase perched on top of the chute ready to hurtle down. Stacia prayed it wouldn't open again, could envision too clearly her underwear cannoning down and circling round and round on top of other people's baggage. When her suitcase had successfully navigated the drop, she let out her breath slowly.

'Got anything to hide?'

She whirled around and found Andrew's blue gaze fixed intently on her face.

'Greek customs' officials are amongst the toughest in the world,' he added.

She frowned, didn't answer, and moved away through the crowd to retrieve her bag. She heaved it off the carousel, then looked for Andrew again. Couldn't see him.

Seemed impossible he'd been faster than her, but if she didn't see him again, it would save any need for final words. His disappearance felt funny though, made the trip feel unfinished. Especially as he'd suggested they get together in Athens. Disconcerting, how disappointed she felt that they wouldn't.

A man lunged for his bag as it swept around the carousel away from him. Stacia shifted sideways, made her way out of the path of those still collecting their luggage, and headed with other passengers towards the customs' desk.

Once through customs, she would hit the tourist bureau. No, the hotel first, where she would find Mr. Andropolous's son and get rid of the package.

A large woman with damp patches under her arms suddenly blocked Stacia's way. They both danced crazily in an effort to get around each other. The large woman smiled and gestured to her right, then glanced over Stacia's shoulder, and her eyes widened.

There was no time to turn, no time to think. A flash of light, a sudden roar, and Stacia's world burst apart.

3

The blast swept Stacia off her feet and flung her like a rag doll sideways into the crowd. The large woman flew with her, their limbs entwined in a tangled web of soft flesh and hard bones. With a painful thump, they landed together on the ground.

The air fled Stacia's lungs. The suffocating smell of acrid smoke filled the space left behind.

Madness erupted. Muted confusion became screams of terror. Moans and piteous crying swelled to the high-pitched keening of the wounded.

Andrew. His image wobbled in and out of Stacia's consciousness, piercing the fog surrounding her brain. She lifted her head, and a pain unconnected to broken bones or punctured skin penetrated her soul.

She couldn't bear for it to happen,

for death to strike her life again so soon. She didn't love Andrew as she had loved her father, but she wouldn't *allow* him to be dead.

He had to have been behind her, somewhere closer to the blast. She struggled to rise, but something heavy lay across her shoulders. She curled her fingers into fists and pushed her upper body from the ground. The person on top groaned, and flopped to one side.

Other passengers raised their heads, and gazed around, also, their hands reaching for the reassuring presence of loved ones. She couldn't see Andrew. Stacia sucked in a breath of air and struggled to beat back her fear.

Other people slowly stood and clutched at family members, picked up their suitcases, and swiftly moved away. It was as though another bomb, if that's what the explosion had been, was about to blow them up at any moment.

Stacia got to her feet and glanced toward the luggage carousel. It was a twisted mass of jagged metal, covered in and surrounded by scraps of fluttering material. Suitcases full of clothes had been flung high by the blast and lay scattered like broken matchsticks, their contents exposed and incongruously normal amongst the chaos. Stacia forced her way toward the carousel, fighting against an ever-increasing tide of panic-stricken passengers going in the opposite direction.

'Andrew,' she called, her cry a croaked whisper.

Alarms went off, some loud and strident, others with the mind-numbing syncopation of police sirens.

Uniformed officials, their faces white and strained, pushed their way through the crowd. They commanded in loud voices that those passengers who were able should move to the left side of the customs' lounge quickly and quietly.

'Andrew!' Stacia shouted again, louder this time.

'Stacia!'

She heard him call her name before his hand touched her shoulder. She swung around to face him, found his eyes two bottomless wells of blue, and his arms a haven. With a muffled cry, she fell into his embrace and wrapped herself in his comforting warmth.

She stood against him trembling, stunned by the enormity of her relief. He clung to her as tightly, the heat from his body penetrating the chill encasing her own. Vaguely, she became aware of the official again, who was urging them both to move.

Embarrassed, she pulled herself away from Andrew's arms. 'I thought you'd been killed,' she mumbled.

'I'm glad you care,' he said softly.

'Of course, I care.' She didn't look at him, stared instead at the chaos surrounding them.

'Come on,' he said gently, putting his arm around her shoulders. 'Let's get out of here.'

★ ★ ★

Getting out of there would have taken longer if Andrew hadn't smoothed the way, Stacia admitted to herself ruefully. He had located her suitcases as well as his own and had led Stacia to where they were supposed to go. On the way, he had helped others; a woman and her child, an old man dazed and staggering. Despite the confusion engulfing the hall, they had been processed, their passports stamped, and their bags passed back to them.

The police, a special emergency squad by the looks of their uniforms, had watched the customs officers work. They had eyed each passenger suspiciously and demanded addresses of where they could be reached in Athens.

Andrew's eyebrows lifted when Stacia gave the name of the Hotel Athena. *Not* staying with friends, the compressed line of his mouth seemed to say.

But none of that mattered, she decided dully, not compared to the explosion and the danger they'd been in, the fact some people were injured, perhaps even killed.

She couldn't tell the full extent of the damage, for the police had erected barriers, screening off the area from passengers' curious stares. When they began to carry out stretchers, she looked away, determined to stop the trembling from beginning again.

Along with the other passengers, she and Andrew were escorted through the yellow-ribboned police lines. The crush was unbelievable, the confusion overwhelming. Joyful greetings took place as terrified relatives hailed emerging passengers. Noisy reunions resulted with everyone talking at once.

The police cleared the building, and directed the crowd out the side doors. Taxis, too, had been diverted away from the main entrance, away from interference with police vehicles and ambulances.

'Wait here,' Andrew instructed. He dropped his bag at Stacia's feet and moved swiftly away. 'I'll get a cab.'

'I — ' Stacia bit back her words. There was no point in calling after him. At least he'd be easier to spot in this country, standing head and shoulders above everyone else.

The taxis were lined up helter-skelter, nose in to the sidewalk. Their prospective passengers were chaotic. People jerked open the doors before the taxi had even stopped and lunged in before someone else got there first.

Stacia felt drained. She yearned for the silence of her hotel room and a long soothing soak in a hot bath. Anything, to push back the images of bombs and destruction.

Images of Andrew, also.

With a frown, she dumped her bags on top of his, not able to go her own way while watching his luggage as well as her own. She could see him now, crouched over and speaking to one of the taxi drivers, then all at once he straightened, and waved in her direction.

He smiled like a small boy bringing home a prize, making it difficult to hang on to her annoyance. Stacia averted her face to hide her answering smile, and stared at the crowd instead. People choked the sidewalk, pushing and shoving in their eagerness to depart. Except for a couple strolling towards her, who seemed to have no business at the airport at all. They had no luggage, no air of purpose.

The horror of the bomb still sat inside Stacia's brain ready to explode a second time. She mustn't think about the bombing now, mustn't look at every person passing as though they were the bombers themselves. She rolled her shoulders in a vain attempt to loosen her tension.

The couple drew closer. The woman's jeans were frayed, the holes in the knees beyond repair. Probably the leader of fashion in her own circle of friends.

Someone bumped against Stacia and she pulled her luggage closer, straddling the largest suitcase with her legs before glancing again at the unkempt couple.

The woman's companion ran grimy fingers through his uncombed hair. His gaze shifted from side to side, not resting on anything.

49

Some defense mechanism inside Stacia jarred to life. She slung her purse around her neck and clutched its strap, meanwhile tightening her legs around her suitcase. The couple parted as they approached her, the man going left, and the woman right.

Close up, the expression in the man's eyes made Stacia's skin crawl. Goose bumps erupted on her neck and traveled across her shoulders. She twisted around to follow his movement, not trusting to lift her gaze from his deliberate saunter. Then with a suddenness that stunned, he began to run.

A sudden slash of a knife disturbed the air on Stacia's right, creating a breeze, an instant of cold. Her purse fell from her shoulder, and the woman was now running, holding in her hand, Stacia's purse. The strap the woman had cut dragged on the floor after her.

The air fled Stacia's lungs. She screamed in protest, but the sound of her scream was as inaudible as the cry of a gull in the face of a storm.

Untangling her feet, she chased after the couple.

The next time she screamed, people heard her. But the man and woman were elusive, darting and dodging so swiftly, onlookers had no time to react.

Stacia tried to run faster but the only feeling in her legs was numbness. She might have been moving in slow motion, she made so little progress. There were no guards here to help her, and no police. They were all inside the airport, dealing with a disaster much more serious than a stolen purse.

Rage surged through her. There had been too much taking. Taking purses, taking lives. It had to stop. Suddenly Stacia heard footsteps thundering behind. Irrationally, terror replaced the rage, and engulfed her as though she were the one pursued.

She couldn't breathe. Couldn't think. Didn't want to think.

The footsteps drew closer, but she couldn't run any faster. There were too many people. Her throat was raw with the effort of calling out, of simply breathing. Amazingly, the woman appeared in front of her again. Stacia's rage resurfaced. Everything she needed was in that purse — her money, passport, tickets, and hotel vouchers. She lunged for the woman's shirt, but the thief side-stepped and she missed. The man was suddenly there instead and in his hand was another knife.

He slashed at Stacia's face, but she twisted away. The next instant he was gone, and the woman, too.

A hand clamped onto Stacia's shoulder and swung her around.

'What the hell do you think you're doing?' Andrew's eyes blazed into hers.

'They've taken my purse,' she cried. Her hands formed fists and she raised them to Andrew's chest.

'So you chased them? Risked getting killed?'

'Everything I need is in that purse.'

'It's not worth dying over.' His fingers tightened on her shoulder. 'Tell me what happened.'

'Two people . . . a man . . . a woman.' She struggled to think clearly. 'The man looked so . . . dangerous.' An uncontrollable spasm shook her entire body.

Andrew grabbed hold of her other shoulder and drew his hands down the length of her arms. She crossed her arms in front of her, unsettled by his touch.

'The woman — '

'Slowly. Just tell me slowly.' He touched her again, but lightly, as though to gentle her.

'The woman took my purse. Cut the strap. Pulled on it.' She glared at him. 'If I hadn't been anchored with all that luggage . . . '

Andrew glanced critically at her waist. 'Travel rule number three, Ms Roberts, you should have worn a money belt.'

'Well, I didn't.' Though the guide books had made that recommendation, too. She had planned to buy a leather one in Athens. 'Just go away,' she muttered, furious with herself.

'And leave you here alone?'

'Yes!'

'You need me.'

'I do *not* need you.'

'How do you plan to pay for a taxi into Athens?'

Her stomach lurched sickeningly.

'Do you have money stashed anywhere else?'

'No.'

'Traveler's cheques?'

Wordlessly, she shook her head. The cash in the envelope had been enough. She hadn't bothered with traveler's cheques.

She had money in the bank back home, but to send for it would take time. Besides, it was the weekend. No banks were open. The sick feeling intensified. Her hotel vouchers were gone, along with her passport, bank card, and credit cards.

'I wouldn't count on getting anything back,' Andrew said. 'In the meantime — '

Her ears buzzed.

' — you'd better come with me.'

'Come with *you?*' she repeated incredulously.

'I don't see you have much choice.'

The sick feeling deepened to desperation.

'We'll report the theft to the police,' he said, taking her by the arm, 'then check into a hotel. But we'll get our luggage first. Better hope it's still there.'

Stacia stifled a gasp. Mr. Andropolous's package was in her suitcase. Her clothes she could afford to lose. She couldn't lose the package.

An old woman was sitting on Stacia's suitcase when they returned, her own small bundle at her feet and a crooked wooden cane lying menacingly across her lap. When she caught sight of Stacia, she smiled and stood. Andrew thrust his hand into his pocket and pulled out an American ten dollar bill. With an emphatic shake of her head, the woman melted away into the crowd.

Two airport guards, too late to catch

the thieves, emerged at last from the now near empty airport. With their stern and tense expressions, they looked as impossible to approach as any villain. Fatigue washed over Stacia, but she took a bag in each hand and stuck close to Andrew as he pushed his way toward the guards.

★ ★ ★

'I'm booked at the Hotel Athena,' Stacia said wearily, when finally she and Andrew climbed into a cab.

'So you told the police before. Why did you lie to *me?*'

'Surely you know why! It's probably one of your rules! Never let on to strangers where you are staying.'

He didn't answer.

'It's only for a night or two.' Once she got rid of the package, she would move somewhere else.

'Why the Athena?' Andrew watched her closely through narrow eyes.

'I have to meet someone there.' Mr.

Stone had said tell no one, but Mr. Stone hadn't figured she would lose all her money. The inside of Stacia's cheek felt raw from chewing.

'The Athena's expensive.'

'I'll pay you back.' If it took every cent in her savings account. 'My bank will be open Monday and I'll phone the U.S. Embassy. They probably have an aid fund for stranded travelers.'

Andrew shrugged, then leaned forward and gave the taxi driver the name of the Athena.

★ ★ ★

Stacia tilted her head backward, but still couldn't see every detail of the vaulted ceiling. All of Mount Olympus could have fit into the Athena's lobby, and after the too-fast, blistering hot taxi ride, the hotel's cool, tomb-like interior felt wonderfully peaceful. She hadn't dared shut her eyes in the taxi, convinced that if she did, they would never make it to their destination alive.

There was no sign of Andropolous's son. She had hoped he would be here when she arrived, relaxing in one of the lobby's deep-cushioned chairs. She cast another glance around. There were people in the lobby, but none of them seemed to be looking for her. Though Andropolous's son might not realize she was the courier. He wouldn't be expecting her to be accompanied by a man.

Perhaps he had left her a message. Stacia moved toward the reception desk where Andrew stood frowning at the clerk.

'I'm sorry, sir,' the clerk said, 'but it's the best I can do.'

'Then it will have to do,' Andrew replied grimly, looking suddenly as weary as Stacia felt. He scrawled something on the register and turned to face her. 'Ready?'

'You've registered already?' She glanced at the clerk. 'Are there any messages for me? My name's Stacia Roberts.'

'Roberts?' The clerk cast Andrew a puzzled glance.

'Her maiden name,' Andrew explained swiftly. 'We're newlyweds. Come along, darling.' Unexpectedly, he took Stacia by the arm and brushed her cheek with his lips.

Stacia raised her hand to her cheek, her heart suddenly pounding.

'Just play along,' Andrew whispered, his lips now skimming her ear. 'If they get any messages for you, darling,' he said, speaking louder, 'they'll send them on up.' He glanced inquiringly at the clerk.

'Certainly, sir. Immediately.'

Stacia tried to pull her arm away. Andrew's grip tightened.

'What's going on?' Had he gone mad?

He followed the porter toward the elevator, pulling her along with him. 'I'll explain when we get to the room,' he murmured, not looking crazy, simply out of sorts.

The porter halted in front of the wrought iron doors of an ancient elevator. An ornate metal cage swept toward them from above and settled to a halt with a gentle hiss.

The door slid open and the pressure of Andrew's fingers on Stacia's elbow increased. She snatched her arm free and stepped into the elevator. She'd follow Andrew's lead for the moment, but he'd better have a damned good explanation.

On the sixth floor, the elevator shuddered to a stop. The porter led the way down a plushly carpeted hall to a pair of double doors. When he swung them wide open, Stacia stared into the room.

This hotel *was* expensive. Ornate antique furniture rested on Persian carpets, and marble fixtures gleamed from the bathroom beyond. But it was the view that must have cost the earth. Across the intervening roof tops, the white columns of the Parthenon climbed toward the sky.

With difficulty, Stacia pulled her gaze from the magic of antiquity. *Andrew* didn't seem in the least bit stunned by the hotel's grandeur. He carelessly slipped the porter some money and shut the door behind him.

'Why did you lie about us being married?' Stacia demanded.

'To get us a room,' Andrew replied cryptically. He unzipped his bag and dumped its contents on the bed, then heaved her bag up beside his.

'We're not *both* staying here?' she croaked, suddenly nervous now that the porter had left her alone with a mad man.

'Yup.'

'But where — '

'There's plenty of space.' He grabbed a pile of shirts and placed them in the bottom drawer of the dresser.

'If you think for one minute — '

He turned to her, and grinned. 'Just think of it as protecting your honor.'

'My *honor?*'

'They needed a passport for registration and you don't have yours. It was simpler to say you were with me.'

'Simpler?' Andrew's eyes seemed bluer than ever. Blue. Brown. White slave trader's eyes came in all colors according to her father.

'There didn't seem any other choice.' Andrew shrugged and turned away. He picked up a bundle of shorts and pants, and dropped them in the drawer next to his shirts.

'I must have my own room,' Stacia stated firmly. Andrew might be a man used to making decisions, but he wasn't deciding for her. Sitting next to him on the plane had been difficult enough, sharing a room was unthinkable.' Couldn't we get a suite with two adjoining bedrooms? That wouldn't require me showing a passport.'

He carried his shaving gear into the bathroom.

'If it's the money you're worried about — '

He came out again, his bulk filling the bathroom doorway. 'It's not the money.'

'What then?'

'I don't *know* you,' he said softly, 'but somehow you've become my responsibility.'

'You are *not* responsible for me! The embassy — ' His smile stopped her.

'Whether you'll admit it or not,' he said, 'you have no money, no passport, and no ticket out of here. I have all three and I don't mind sharing.' One brow lifted. 'So seeing as how I'm investing in you,' he added slowly, 'I'm sticking to you like glue.'

Stacia stared at him in disbelief.

'Besides,' he continued, a dimple flashing onto his chin, 'this was the last vacancy they had in the place. *Your* reservation seems to have vanished with the wind.' He glanced appreciatively around the room before turning back to her. 'Welcome to the honeymoon suite.'

4

Stacia stared past Andrew to the far side of the room, her gaze drawn irresistibly to the king-sized bed covered in quilts and fluffy pillows.

A love nest. Ideal for honeymooners.

Which she and Andrew Moore *were* *not*.

Her cheeks hot, she tugged her gaze away from the bed. 'We can't stay here together.'

Andrew shrugged. 'Up to you.'

Stacia sucked in a breath. He knew damn well she had no place else to go.

His lips twisted upward. 'We're both adults, Stacia. I didn't think this would be a problem.'

'If you think — '

'You keep your distance and I'll keep mine.'

'Fine.' She drew in a deep breath. 'You take the couch and I'll take the bed.' That ought to dispel any notions he might have.

'How about we toss for it?' He slipped off his shirt and pulled a cotton sweater from the drawer. 'That couch is pretty damn short — '

'Live with it,' she said. Her heart pounded furiously. 'This was *your* idea, remember.'

'Fine,' he said, the word muffled as he pulled his sweater over his head.

His chest was as broad in the flesh as it had appeared fully clothed. A line of black hair drew Stacia's gaze up from the waistband of his pants to the curly hair covering his chest.

Unsought sensations blasted through her, bringing heat to Stacia's face. She pressed her lips together and turned away, determined to ignore what she was feeling, furious with herself for being so shy. It just seemed too personal, too intimate, standing next to a bed in a strange country with a man she had just met.

A tap sounded at the door. With a

sense of relief, Stacia moved to open it. Andrew got there first, his sweater scarcely settled over his bare skin.

Two policemen stood in the doorway, their legs apart, their feet resting solidly on the floor.

'Yes, officers?' Andrew said politely.

The policeman with a pencil-thin moustache consulted his note pad. 'Mr. Moore?' he said, glancing up at Andrew.

'Yes.'

'And Miss Roberts?'

'Yes.' She moved forward eagerly. 'Have you found my purse?'

'Your purse?' The officer seemed puzzled.

'It was stolen this morning. At the airport,' Stacia added impatiently. 'The guard we reported it to said he would get in touch with us if there was any word.'

'We're not airport guards,' the taller policeman said firmly, his accent thick, but his English good. He pulled out his identification card and held it toward them. 'We're with the special unit investigating the bombing.'

'Do you know who was responsible?' Stacia asked, capturing her bottom lip between her teeth. The horror of the airport explosion again filled her mind.

'No terrorist group has come forward, yet,' the policeman said. His stern expression told them that he'd be the one asking the questions.

'What can *we* do for you?' Andrew asked. He opened the door wider and motioned the officers into the room.

'We have a few questions.' The tall officer moved to the couch and sat down, pulling the coffee table closer and placing his notebook on it. 'We have reason to believe the intended target was one of our government's ministers. He was booked on your flight. Fortunately, his travel plans were altered.' The officer flipped his notebook open to a clean page, and pulled out a pen. 'We'd like a copy of your itinerary, addresses of where you'll be staying in Greece, and the purpose of your trip to our country.'

There was little written on Stacia's page when the officer had completed her statement. She didn't have a set plan, intending simply to drift after completing her courier job and find a sunsoaked island with plenty of ruins.

Andrew's responses were no more revealing than her own. 'Will that be all?' he asked.

'Unless you have anything else you want to tell us.' When neither replied, the mustached officer asked, 'Did you see anyone acting suspiciously?'

Stacia shook her head. 'That's what made it so unbelievable, that life could be so normal, then explode without warning into horror.'

She added quietly. 'We saw the stretchers. Did anyone — ' She bit her lip. ' — die?'

'Two,' the policeman said, his whiskers bristling. 'So far,' he added.

Stacia drew in a shaky breath. Andrew's jaw tightened and his eyes seemed to unfocus, as though he stared inward at something he couldn't bear to see.

Then the officer spoke again. 'Did you see anyone bring anything on board the aircraft that didn't seem to belong to them?'

The heat spread across Stacia's cheeks. *She* had something that didn't belong to her. In her own suitcase lay a package wrapped in brown paper and tied up with string. Wordlessly, she shook her head, no.

'Did *you* bring anything into the country not belonging to you?' the policeman asked.

'No,' she lied again, praying her face wouldn't betray her. She'd been told what was in the package, but she didn't *know*. It had never occurred to her to look. Couriers transported packages all the time without actually seeing the contents of what they carried.

The policeman's eyes watched her, his gaze narrowed.

Stacia's throat tightened. She couldn't tell him now about the package. She'd read about smugglers and the hard line the courts took. Locked up for years in a foreign jail. She shuddered. If it turned out to be drugs, the police would never believe her innocence.

'Well, officers,' Andrew said, moving toward the door and opening it, 'if there's nothing else?'

Stacia's pulse raced faster. It was difficult to keep from glancing toward her suitcase.

'That's all for the moment,' the taller officer said, flipping his notebook shut, 'but call if you think of anything else.'

Andrew moved between her and the policemen, blocking the rest of what the officer said. Then the men moved through into the hall and Andrew gently shut the door behind them. He turned to her, his eyes hard and unrelenting.

'You lied,' he accused.

'Let's get one thing straight.' Stacia gritted her jaw. 'You stay out of my business and I'll stay out of yours.'

'As long as you're with me, your

business *is* my business.' He drew closer to her. 'I have no intention of going to jail on your account.'

'Then you've got nothing to worry about.'

He examined her face for an instant more, then released her gaze so abruptly, she staggered. 'I'm going out for a newspaper.' He grabbed up a baseball cap from the bottom of his suitcase, and jammed it on his head. He closed the door quietly as he left, but the sound echoed in Stacia's head long after he was gone.

She counted to twenty, then forty, wanting to be sure Andrew wouldn't come back when she least expected him. Then slowly, tentatively, she walked over to her suitcase and unclasped the latches. The package rested near the top, partially covered by her new silk blouse.

Stacia took a deep breath and pulled the package out, pushing away her reluctance to open mail that wasn't hers. For a long moment, she stared at it, the name Andropolous blackly accusing. Finally, knowing she had to do it, she eased open the tape and pulled the contents from the wrapping paper.

One sweater, black, soft and feminine, fell into her hands. On top of it was a sealed envelope, again with the name Andropolous in clear, black print.

Exactly as Mr. Stone had said.

As heady as sunshine on a rainy day, relief filled Stacia's heart. With trembling fingers, she carefully re-folded the sweater and placed it and the envelope back in the wrapping. She stuck the tape back around it and buried the package at the bottom of her suitcase.

Minutes later, Andrew returned.

'Any news on the bombing?' Stacia asked, closing the book she'd been attempting unsuccessfully to read.

'Front page,' Andrew replied tersely. 'A third passenger died in the hospital. They're saying a right-wing terrorist group is responsible, but there's no confirmation.'

At least *her* package had nothing to do with the bombing. It contained exactly what she'd been told.

Stacia jumped as a tap sounded at the door. She never used to be nervous, had gone to work each day at the library knowing she'd come home again in the evening. A change from order and calm was what she had desired from this trip, but she hadn't expected this.

Andrew once again reached the door before she did. It was the hotel porter this time. Andrew took the proffered note, reached into his pocket and, from a seemingly unlimited supply of cash, handed the young man a tip.

'Is it from the airport police?' Stacia asked anxiously. 'Have they found my purse?'

He slowly turned over the envelope and read the lettering on the front.

Stacia fought the urge to snatch it from his hand.

'It's for you,' he finally said. With a thoughtful glance in her direction, he held it out.

Stacia took the paper and turned away to read it.

'Is it from your . . . *friend?*'

'Yes.'

'Well?'

'He's not going to be able to meet me here today after all.' She lowered her gaze, tried to hide her disappointment.

'He?'

'Does it matter?' she inquired coldly, meeting his gaze now.

'You don't seem the type to meet a man in an expensive hotel half way around the world.'

He'd called her beautiful before and *now* she wasn't the type.

'You don't know anything about me,' she said.

'True,' he agreed, frowning.

'So how can you possibly make that kind of assessment?'

His lips curved into a half-smile. 'I've got eyes.'

Stacia drew herself up to her full height. 'What does that mean?' she demanded.

His gaze swept over her assessingly. He frowned. 'You're not dressed like an expensive toy.'

Nothing she owned was expensive. Unless you counted the book she'd bought on her twenty-first birthday, a leather bound edition of Kazantzakis' *Zorba The Greek*. If any man had made her want to visit Greece, it was the famous author — not some rich old fool existing only in the imagination of Andrew Moore.

'Are you quite through?' she asked icily.

'I meant it as a compliment,' he said, his expression softening. He stepped closer. 'I told you before you were beautiful, and I meant it.'

She stepped backward.

'When is your friend meeting you?'

'He doesn't say.' Her fingers formed a fist around the note in her hand, and she crushed its message away from Andrew's inquisitive eyes.

'How well do you know this man?'

'That's none of your business.'

'You've made it my business.'

'What do you mean?'

'I'm hardly going to leave you alone in a strange country, with no money — '

'I told you I would pay you back.'

' — and no passport.' He glanced at the crumpled paper in her hand. 'You might get into trouble and not be able to get out.'

'So I'm supposed to depend on you to keep me safe?'

'You could do worse.'

'I know nothing about you, and according to you, strangers are synonymous with axe murderers.'

'Now you've got it.' A crinkling around his eyes spread to a grin on his lips.

She took another step backward, only stopping when the back of her knees bumped the edge of the bed.

'If we're going to be room-mates,' Andrew went on softly, 'we'd better get to know each other.'

Stacia forgot to breathe.

He smiled down at her, his eyes bluer than any man's had a right to be. 'Can I take you to dinner?' he asked.

* ★ ★ ★

Now was the time to go. When he wouldn't hear her movements above the sound of his shower. Stacia shook her head, tried to force away the image of Andrew under the spray, the water hitting his hard body and dripping down its length.

He hadn't left her alone all afternoon. They'd eyed each other warily, had taken turns making phone calls. Hers, to her bank, closed, as she had known it would be, and to her friend, Angela, gone for the weekend according to the cheery voice on the answering machine. It hardly mattered. Her friend had no money to send her anyway. She had called more from a desire to hear Angela's voice, in the hopes it would dispel the apprehension building within.

His call was to the airport, checking with security as to whether her bag had been recovered. A rueful shake of his head told her the answer. Then another call, or two, with his back turned towards her, Andrew's shower water didn't stop. Was the open bathroom door a mistake? An invitation? Stacia grimaced. Most likely, he'd left it open to keep her in view.

Thank goodness, the carpet was thick. Her feet made no sound as she tiptoed across the room. She collected the tote bag Andrew had bought for her when he'd gone out for a paper, the tote bag now holding her parcel. Moving to the door, she pushed the handle down and pulled.

It opened noiselessly. Well oiled. Well maintained. A luxury hotel down to the smallest detail. One last glance toward the bathroom and she was in the hall.

She avoided the elevator and took the stairs. With Andrew liable to appear at any moment to stare over the balustrade, she didn't want to be trapped in the elevator cage like a lamb roasting on a spit. Shoving her hand into her pocket, she pulled out the crumpled paper and re-read its message beneath the dull light of the stairwell.

Miss Roberts,
Meet me at Greco Taverna, 7:00 p.m.
Andropolous

Apprehension flared. What was wrong with a well-lit hotel lobby? Mr. Stone had implied Andropolous was eccentric, but there were limits.

Stacia pushed open the door at the bottom of the stairs and emerged next to the front desk. A quick chat with the concierge, a winding line drawn on a multi-colored tourist map, and she was ready. She walked out the front door and into the night.

Athens' streets were darker than those back home. If she'd had money, she'd have taken a taxi. Even without, she managed the first two blocks confidently. Tourists were everywhere, and she blended into the crowd. The next two blocks were different. She stood out from the throng of locals. Her coloring was almost right, but her clothes, her bearing, everything else cried foreigner.

As she paused in the doorway of a shop, a group of young men sauntered past. They preened themselves in the shop window and gestured widely to each other.

Stacia stared at the goods displayed behind the window and tried not to feel nervous of the men still so close. It was a difficult task since the bombing this morning and the snatching of her purse by a thief.

When the men continued on, she peeked into the street. Nobody was approaching but a couple of giggling girls, strolling side by side, arm in arm. How wonderful it would be if she could insert herself between them and walk to the taverna with a buffer on either side. The desk clerk had said the taverna was close, but it already seemed as though she'd been walking for miles.

With a sigh, she consulted her map, then stepped back onto the narrow sidewalk. A sharp left took her to a street winding steeply up a hill. The sign *Greco Taverna* swung just ahead, the stark white columns of the Parthenon depicted upon it. Not many people around now — almost more frightening than before.

She glanced over her shoulder, but no one was there. She'd experienced the eeriest sensation since leaving the hotel that someone was following her. Was she becoming paranoid as well as nervous? The sooner she got rid of the package, the better.

With a tightening of her lips, she opened the door to the taverna. It was darker inside than out. The only light came from candles stuck unceremoniously in the top of wine bottles and placed in the center of each table.

As Stacia stared around the room, her dismay increased. It was so crowded. How on earth was she supposed to know which man was Andropolous? Most of the customers appeared to be locals. The few tourists stood out, recognizable from the camera bags propped at the foot of their chairs, the colorful shawls clinging to the shoulders of the women, and the pullover shirts covering the chests of the men. The windows of the craft shops were filled with such clothing.

Of the Greek patrons, nothing much distinguished one man from the next — a fuller mustache, a black cap tilted back rather than forward, fierce black eyes and ones that frankly appraised.

It was impossible. She would never find Andropolous unless he approached her.

Suddenly a man at the back of the room, Greek, from the looks of him, scraped his chair away from the table. Black hair touched with grey gleamed from beneath his cap and his pants were tight, revealing muscular thighs and a fit man's stance.

The man wended his way purposefully towards her, squeezing between the crowded tables. Instinctively, Stacia clutched her bag more tightly.

Cool night air hit her bare legs as the door behind her opened. Without warning, strong fingers caught her arm. She whirled around.

Andrew.

His gaze locked with hers, his blue eyes turning black in the light.

And *angry*.

Stacia jerked free and again faced the Greek man. He was closer now, but no longer looking at her. He stared past her, toward Andrew, then suddenly pushed the chair nearest him out of the way, nearly knocking an elderly man to the floor in the process. Twisting and turning, he elbowed through the diners, moving away from both her and Andrew.

Stacia sank into an empty chair as Andrew pushed his way past her. His muffled oath sounded harsh in her ear. Andrew swept through the taverna in pursuit of the stranger, while she looked on in disbelief.

The man raced past the bar towards the kitchen, sparing one swift glance over his shoulder at the bag in Stacia's arms. With a scowl, he shoved a chair into Andrew's path, then disappeared into the kitchen amid the excited clamor of the cook.

Andrew flung the chair aside and proceeded after him. Metal clattered, men yelled, and doors slammed, until, at last, there was nothing left but silence.

Stacia slowly let out her breath. From the lack of sound in the small room, she was not the only one who'd been holding it. Then, in a flood, everyone began talking at once. A few men stood, as though intending to join the chase, but at the exhortations of their friends, sank back into their chairs.

'Are you all right, my dear?'

Dry, cool fingers patted Stacia's hand. She tore her gaze from the spot Andrew and the man had disappeared, and looked across the table. Mild blue eyes set in a berry brown face stared back at her.

'Here, have my tea . . . I haven't poured it, yet,' the woman continued, her voice as comforting as the lilac perfume she wore

Stacia's grandmother had worn lilac perfume. The scent had soothed Stacia when she was young, and it soothed her now. She nodded her assent and the elderly woman opposite poured the tea into a cup. She spooned in four or five teaspoons of sugar, far too much to be palatable.

'Sugar for shock,' the older woman said firmly. She pushed the cup toward Stacia. 'My name is Mary Argyle.' She held out her hand. 'You may call me Mary. And you are?'

'Stacia Roberts.' It seemed unreal to be exchanging names when Andrew was out in the night chasing heaven knew who — or why.

'Very pleased to meet you, my dear,' Mary replied primly. 'Now tell me. What on earth was that all about?'

'I'm not sure,' Stacia said uncertainly.

'Your young man certainly seemed angry.'

'He's *not* my young man.'

'Oh?' Mary Argyle's slightly opaque eyes turned shrewd.

'I . . . I barely know him,' Stacia

stammered. *She didn't know him at all.*

Mary's thin, grey eyebrows rose. 'He seems to know you. He defended you rather gallantly.'

Stacia grimaced. 'Defended me from what?'

'Why, from that other young man, of course.'

'I've never seen *him* before at all.'

'Quite dreadful manners,' Mary said, frowning, 'making such a fuss in a public place. This place came highly recommended, too!'

Stacia relaxed into her chair. The woman opposite was so normal, so reassuring, and her indignation transformed the scene from the frightening to the merely absurd. If it weren't for expecting Andrew to re-emerge as suddenly as he had disappeared, Stacia could almost pretend the chase had never taken place at all. Unexpectedly, she longed to see him.

Mary cocked her head sideways in a manner resembling a grey sparrow. 'Your young man must know him,' she insisted, calmly voicing the thought Stacia hadn't wanted to acknowledge.

If the man was Andropolous's son and Andrew knew him . . . what then? She gulped down a mouthful of the hot tea, trying to get warm, trying not to imagine the worse.

'You're still here. Good.'

Stacia jerked around. Andrew stood behind her, his eyes cold and his jaw set in a harsh line.

'He got away,' he went on, breathing between the words in short, hungry gasps, as though he'd been running the entire time he'd been gone. 'It's as black as Hades out there.'

'Why did you chase him?' Stacia asked.

'Why did he run?'

Her chest tightened. 'Do you know him?' she demanded hoarsely. *Are you his younger brother?*

Andrew stared at her intently, not allowing her gaze to slip from his, not allowing her a crumb of comfort.

'No,' he finally answered.

'Then, why?'

'He had a knife — '

'I didn't see a knife.'

' — and he looked as though he meant to use it.' A muscle twitched above his right eye. 'I was protecting you! Trying to keep you safe.'

Stacia's cheeks flared hot. 'You're not my keeper.'

'Someone has to do it.'

'Not *you*.' She wrapped her arms around her body. 'Not *anyone*.'

'Was he your friend?' he asked, ignoring her words.

'No!' she exclaimed. Though he might have been. Either that or the younger of Andropolous's sons. But if he was the younger son, that meant Andrew wasn't. She shook her head, tried to clear her confusion. 'Why did he run when he saw you?' she asked, not sure that Andrew would tell her the truth.

'That's what I'm asking *you!*'

'Sit down, both of you, and have some tea.' Mary Argyle's voice was soothing, unruffled.

Stacia had forgotten for a moment the older woman was there.

'We can't stay,' Andrew said. 'We have dinner reservations.'

'We don't — '

His gaze bore into Stacia's. 'This afternoon, you agreed to have dinner with me.'

She stared back at him, undecided. Maybe it would be best to go to dinner with Andrew, find out who and what he was. Slowly, she nodded.

Andrew turned and smiled at Mary. 'Perhaps another time, Mrs . . . ?'

'Argyle,' Mary said, her eyelids fluttering. 'That would be lovely.' She turned to Stacia. 'Where are you staying, dear?'

'The Hotel Athena.'

'Very nice.'

'We enjoy it.' Unexpectedly, Andrew grinned.

'I'm sure,' Mary said, smiling primly at them both. 'You're having dinner there, I take it.'

'Yes,' Andrew replied.

'Good,' Mary said, looking relieved. 'You're aware then that you have to be off the streets by eight o'clock.'

'What do you mean?' Andrew demanded.

'Because of the bombing this morning at the airport — '

'Yes,' he prompted.

' — Martial Law has been declared.'

5

'Martial Law!' Andrew's fingers tightened around Stacia's arm. 'How do you know?'

'It was in the evening paper.'

'We didn't see that edition,' he said grimly.

Stacia peered at her watch. 'It's already seven-thirty.' She glanced worriedly around. The crowd had thinned out. While they had been talking, customers had been leaving. Waiters hustled around the empty tables, cleared the dishes, brushed off the crumbs, exchanged dirty table cloths for clean.

'Goodness,' Mary fluttered, struggling to her feet, 'is that the time already? I only intended to stay a moment, have a quick cup of tea and a rest for my feet. I've been sight-seeing all day.'

'Where are you staying?' Andrew asked. 'We'll escort you home.'

Mary smiled gently. 'How nice, but my hotel is just around the corner. You'll be late if you take me back.'

'Never mind.' He pulled a chair aside so Mary could get out from behind the table. 'You shouldn't be walking the streets alone.'

'We'll take you.' Stacia agreed.

They hurried out of the taverna into the darkened street. Stacia was glad when Andrew kept his hand on her arm. It felt safer, and for once, she liked the feeling.

Miss Argyle seemed happy, too, for their company. She crooked her cane over one hand and contentedly placed her other arm through Andrew's. They made their way up the hill toward the Acropolis, then turned to their left.

'Hurry now,' Miss Argyle admonished them from the doorway of her hotel. She glanced up the street. 'You really should be taking a taxi, but there doesn't seem — '

'Don't worry,' Andrew said, 'we'll make it on time.'

'What will happen if we don't?' Stacia asked, hurrying to keep pace with Andrew's longer stride.

The expression in Andrew's eyes was grim. 'They've probably got the army out if they're serious about patrolling a big city like Athens. If we're caught, they could be nasty, would likely detain us first and ask questions later. I was in Istanbul when a similar thing happened and I — ' Andrew shook his head as if to dispel the memories, and increased his pace.

The cobbled street was dark and empty. Eerie, after being so crowded earlier.

The Parthenon suddenly loomed ahead, its white columns like sentinels at the gates of heaven.

Stacia sucked in a deep breath and slowed her steps. The ruins seemed bathed in magic. She could smell it in the air and hear it in the whispers of the breeze; could see it in the smooth contours of the sculptures scattered about the ancient plaza.

Andrew's steps slowed also. 'The Parthenon was built for Athena.' He looked up at it, admiration in his eyes. 'She was a warrior. A beauty, the myths say — ' His expression softened and the strong lines of his face relaxed. ' — like you.'

He'd called her beautiful before, but the way he said it this time, the way he stared into her eyes, it seemed as though he might kiss her. Stacia's breath caught. If he did, she might like it.

He leaned toward her, and for a long moment, his lips were close. Then a cloud swept in front of the moon, throwing Andrew's face into shadow.

He jerked away. 'We'd better get a move on.' With a long step forward, he separated himself from her.

Stacia remained where she was, frozen to the spot.

Andrew paused, then slowly, almost reluctantly, held out his hand. 'Come on,' he said softly.

Like the whisper of a ghost's passing, urgency swept away the unexpected desire that had surged through Stacia. She took hold of Andrew's hand and together they plunged down the dark, empty, cobblestone street.

The stores were shuttered, and the tavernas empty. Signs swung forlornly above doorways in a breeze sweeping up from nowhere. There were no groups of young men boldly eying the girls. There was no one at all. Even the tourists were gone, no doubt hidden behind locked hotel room doors waiting for morning.

'It's eerie,' Stacia whispered.

Andrew's fingers curled around hers.

They rounded a corner and Stacia's heart skipped a beat. There were soldiers on this street, dozens of them, terrifyingly anonymous in their combat fatigues.

As though a single mind connected them, Stacia and Andrew jumped back behind the building on the corner and flattened themselves against the wall.

'What'll we do?' Stacia whispered. Her heart pounded so loudly she was sure the soldiers could hear.

'What time is it?' Andrew asked.

She peered at her watch. 'Five minutes to eight.' She swallowed hard. Their hotel was at least ten minutes walk away.

A smile tilted the corners of Andrew's mouth, and his eyes held a challenge. 'How fast can you run?' he asked.

'Depends on who's chasing me.' Stacia grinned back at him.

Andrew jerked his thumb toward the soldiers in the next street.

'Fast,' Stacia said.

His smile widened, and he pulled her close. When his lips descended on hers, an impression raced through her of warmth, hardness, and promises postponed.

'You're it,' he said softly, then taking her by the hand, he led her off at a jog in the opposite direction from the soldiers.

Stacia raced beside him. Her legs

pumped and her heart pounded, but whether from the exertion or the kiss, she wasn't sure. She barely knew the man beside her, had no reason to trust him, but however irrational, she was glad he was with her now.

They spotted pockets of soldiers as they fled through the streets, but they zigzagged down the alleyways, avoiding them. Suddenly their hotel came into sight.

A knot of soldiers stood in front of the entrance.

Andrew ducked back into the alleyway, pulling Stacia with him. 'What's the time?' he whispered.

'One minute to go.' Stacia caught her bottom lip between her teeth.

'Come on,' he said firmly. Still holding her hand, he stepped out of the alley and walked briskly toward the hotel entrance.

The soldiers straightened, their gazes narrowing. It might have been an illusion, but Stacia was certain their grips tightened around their rifles.

'Evening,' Andrew said, ignoring the soldiers' guns. He seemed to pretend their presence was normal.

Stacia waited for the order to halt, imagined as she and Andrew mounted the hotel steps, a rifle barrel thrust into her back. Each inch of ground they covered seemed suddenly a mile. Andrew's face was a cool mask, but she could tell by the way his hand tightened around hers that he, too, expected something.

The soldiers did nothing.

Andrew opened the hotel door and nudged Stacia through before him. 'You wanted adventure,' he said, smiling down at her as they crossed the empty lobby.

★   ★   ★

The subdued lighting of the hotel dining room made Andrew's eyes glow like sapphires, and when he smiled again at Stacia, a tingling sensation began in her chest.

She pulled her gaze away and stabbed an olive with her fork. 'I think we should set some guidelines.'

'Guidelines?'

'I did *not* come to Greece for romance.'

'Romance?' Andrew repeated. His eyebrows rose.

Heat crawled up Stacia's throat. 'We kissed, we — '

Andrew leaned forward and for a moment Stacia was certain he meant to kiss her again.

'That wasn't romance,' he said softly, 'that was lust.'

The heat spread to her cheeks. 'Call it what you will, I don't want it. I don't want anything.'

'Nothing?'

'Except a bed, food and some money.' She groaned. 'But I'll pay you back just as soon as my bank opens on Monday.'

'No rush.' His gaze darted to where Stacia's tote bag lay at her feet, then just as swiftly returned to her face.

She pressed her lips tight. Andrew Moore was awfully good at getting what he wanted, and from the way he looked at her package, she could tell he was curious. She nudged her bag with her foot, reassured by its touch, then slowly brought her fork to her mouth. One way or other, she had to find out the truth.

'So what would you like to know — '

Stacia choked. The olive forced its way whole down her throat.

' — my name, rank or serial number?' He gave her a sexy smile.

Her father had once told her all men deceived when they wanted something badly enough. She steeled her heart, and ignored Andrew's smile.

'What work do you do?' she asked.

Andrew hesitated. He had planned what to say, but looking at Stacia now the lie seemed more wrong than stealing. 'I'm a businessman,' he finally managed.

'What kind of business?'

'Small business, small town. Nothing

too exciting.' But in many ways more appealing than the reality. Pain forked through him, still piercing though it was eight years since Nancy had died. He rolled his shoulders, tried to loosen them.

'So what are you doing in Greece?' Stacia asked.

'You asked me that before.'

'I'm asking again.'

'Vacation,' he said, staring straight into her eyes, as a person who was telling the truth would do.

With a sigh, she glanced down again at her bag. The sight of it seemed to spur her on, made her look at him once more, made her frown.

'So what was going on at the taverna?' she demanded.

'Why don't you tell me?'

'You were the one chasing strangers,' she replied hotly. 'You knew him, didn't you?'

'No.' But Andrew could guess what the man was there for and he didn't like the answer.

'Then *why?*' she asked again, slowly, as if to a child. 'Why were you chasing him?'

Andrew somehow managed to remain calm. 'Because he looked as though he meant to do you harm.' Air forced its way rapidly through his clenched teeth. 'Have you forgotten what happened this morning at the airport?'

He watched her flinch, and her eyes dulled from a rich mahogany to a lifeless brown. No, she hadn't forgotten, probably never would.

'The government is taking the bombing seriously enough to proclaim martial law. We should take it at least as seriously.'

'What happened at the airport has nothing to do with us,' she protested.

'I'm sure hoping it doesn't, or have anything to do with the guy with the knife.'

She looked sick. He forced a smile. 'I saved your life. The Chinese philosophers would say I now have an obligation to keep you safe forever.' He reached across the table and took hold of her hand. Her fingers felt icy, and lay in his palm tense, curling inward and away. He began to rub them, wanting to warm them, but glancing into her eyes, he saw the warning.

'Dance with me,' he said instead. He stood, but she didn't move, and for an instant he was sure she would snatch her hand away. But in the end she relented and came into his arms, close enough to touch, too far away to kiss.

He realized with amazement, that a kiss was what he wanted most. To explore her softness with his mouth, taste her essence and breathe her scent. His hand tightened around hers and he watched her lips part, the expression on her face stirring a fierce protectiveness within him. It surged through his veins and built into passion.

Pulling her closer, he found her smaller than she had seemed standing separate from him. And more fragile. He could feel the knobs of her spine as he placed his hand on her back.

There were curves there, as well, beneath her loose fitting dress. A womanly shape. Her hips spread sensuously from her narrow waist, as sumptuous as a Botticelli painting, and as enticing to his hands as her lips were to his mouth.

He gazed at the delicate features of her face. Too thin, he had assumed before. Perfect, he thought now.

She held herself stiffly, her distrust as obvious as the color of her eyes. Brown, with flecks of something darker, yet at the same time, light. Magic eyes.

Eyes that could bewitch.

Her hair matched her eyes. It, too, was brown, but streaked through with red-gold, as though the sun had touched it with its heat. It fell soft as silk around her face, and cascaded against his fingers as his hand trailed up her back.

He shut his eyes, intending to shut out her allure, assuming he wouldn't want what he couldn't see. But her scent embraced him as patently as the violin strains embraced the dancers, urging them to movement with its haunting refrain.

She smelled as she looked, like the earth in all its glory, of a muskiness overlaid with the freshness of flowers. Vibrant spring flowers, full of brilliance and promise. He longed to fill himself with her, to lose himself and his painful memories in her heady scent.

Stifling a groan, he opened his eyes. Her body had lost its stiffness and now melted against his. Her breasts lay crushed against his chest, her nipples hard beneath her dress.

Her nearness drove him mad. He couldn't want her like this, couldn't want her at all.

But he kissed her anyway.

Stacia was unprepared for the need billowing within, for the lips so hard and the kiss so soft. He kissed her lightly at first, as though savoring the first sip of a fine wine. Then he demanded more, his lips exploratory, insistent.

His breath mingled with hers. It was impossible to think, to insist on remaining separate. It was as though they had always been this close, drowning in each other's heat.

Then his lips left hers and he glanced toward their table, toward her tote bag still lying at the foot of her chair.

She felt like a sleeper awakening from a trance. Slowly, stiffly, she pulled away.

'Just making sure your bag is safe,' he explained lightly.

She frowned.

'You don't want to lose anything else.'

'We'd better get going.' She extricated her hand from his.

'You haven't finished your dinner.'

'I'm not hungry.' She stepped away and another dancer's foot came down hard against her heel. Stacia murmured her apologies, not daring another glance into Andrew's compelling eyes, and moved back to their table as swiftly as her throbbing foot would allow. She picked up her bag, feeling relieved at the heaviness within.

Andrew drew close behind her, his warmth encircling hers. She longed to turn and put out her hand, touch the hard line of his shoulders and sink into the comfort of his chest once more. But instead she squared her shoulders and stopped the inclination.

She couldn't want his touch, not believing what she did, not after seeing his expression when he looked at her bag. She wouldn't be free of Andrew until she did the task for which she'd been paid — get the package to Mr. Andropolous's son without further incident.

She turned and faced the hard blue of Andrew's eyes, then together, she and Andrew walked out of the hotel dining room. Side by side, but apart. She felt stiff from the exertion of trying not to touch him, of keeping separate when her body wanted his hands on her skin. As they rode the elevator slowly upward, Stacia's fear grew.

At their room, Andrew inserted his

key into the lock. She hung back while he swung the door wide in front of her. Scarcely breathing, she glanced through the door to the bed beyond. Its hand-woven coverlet was turned down invitingly and the pillows were plumped and ready for use.

He turned to face her, his gaze locking with hers. He didn't speak and she couldn't, but the silence drummed her ears. Nothing moved; not a muscle, not an eyelash . . . nothing. Then, with a swift intake of breath, Andrew moved back into the hall, scarcely touching her as he passed, but close enough for her to feel his heat.

'I'll be back later,' he said curtly. 'Don't wait up.' With that final instruction, he strode down the hall and into the elevator, watching her as the doors closed behind him.

She hadn't realized until then that she'd been holding her breath. It exploded from her lungs in a long drawn out whoosh. She shut the door behind her, but fear trickled through her body's pores, creating a suffocating blackness.

Andrew's leaving solved nothing. He'd come back, and when he did, she'd want him just as fiercely.

★   ★   ★

Her bed sheets were a tangled mess. One more wriggle and the top sheet would come undone altogether. There. It *had*. Wearily, Stacia swung her legs over the side of the bed.

She could scarcely see. A sliver of light shone through from the bathroom, but that was all. Her toe banged up hard against the brass bed frame and she bit her lip to keep from crying out. She walked gingerly to the end of the bed and ripped off the covers. Had to hurry. Andrew might return soon and when he did, she didn't want to be awake.

With a shiver, she wished she had brought her flannel nightie, and hadn't let Angela talk her into buying this silky wisp of nothing. She had told her friend this trip was for discovering the wonders of antiquity, not for waltzing around in see-through black silk. But Angela had smiled cheekily and said you never knew when you'd get lucky.

The illuminated dial of her travel alarm showed two-thirty already. Where could Andrew be? The hotel bar, if that was where he had gone, wouldn't be open all night. Although this was Greece. Who knew what hours they kept?

She flipped the sheet into the air, and held one end tight as it floated back to the bed. Guided by touch, she tucked in the corners. Hospital corners, the kind Grandmother Roberts had taught her to make. Corners that stayed put. Impossible to uproot if you slept properly, her grandmother had told her sternly.

Unlike Stacia's mother's sheets. *She* had flung them on carelessly, laughing at Stacia's suggestion she do them like her grandmother, telling her instead to hang them in the outdoor breeze and capture the scent of the flowers, then tuck them in lightly so the scent could escape. Like sleeping in a flower bed, her mother had insisted, not a jail.

Tonight control was what Stacia needed. She smoothed the blanket flat, her fingers lingering on the nubby woven texture of the edging. With a sudden shiver, she hopped back into bed and pulled the blankets up around her.

It was better than before. Her feet were locked into position as if they were tied. No more tossing and turning and thinking about Andrew. Now she would sleep. Perhaps.

*   *   *

If he kept his eyes averted from the bed, he might just be able to forget she was there. If he didn't see her hair spread out over the pillow, or the soft arch of her brow, it might be possible to banish her from his mind. If he didn't look at her, he might be safe.

But the gentle sound of Stacia's breathing entrapped him as completely as a siren's call. He couldn't force his feet further. It didn't help to tell himself her vulnerability was an act, that she was not someone he needed to protect. Even as he thought it, he couldn't quite believe it, couldn't prevent himself from searching for her in the shadowy light of the moon filtering in through the unshuttered window.

It bathed her face in silver, and her cheeks were flushed, her features more delicate than they had appeared in the light of day. Her eyelids seemed transparent, but still they hid the entrance to her soul.

She didn't look like a woman with secrets, a woman who would lie. Andrew's heart began to pound. She looked like a woman ready for love.

A groan echoed from his lips before he could stifle it. The need to hold her was overwhelming, to crush her to his chest and run his hands over her body, to touch her satin skin and breathe the fragrance of her hair, to taste her nectar, and wrap her in his arms. To keep her safe.

If he could force himself to leave her bedside, the discomfort of the sofa, with it's short length and prickly cover, might be enough to drive all thoughts of love-making from his mind.

He took a step backward, but she moved, also, rolling onto her back. Her hand emerged from beneath her cheek and splayed open on the sheet, her skin a pale cream against the white linen.

His brain ordered his legs to action, but when her lips fluttered open, he paused in mid-stride, mesmerized by the red curve of her mouth, entranced by the soft sigh escaping.

'An . . . drew . . . ' she murmured.

Warmth flooded through him, blocking his intentions and his will. He moved to the edge of the bed, leaned closer in order to hear, was stirred by the sound of his name in her dreams.

She flung her head to one side, the

sound of her moan muffled by her hair. Her neck lay exposed, its slender length both alluring and vulnerable. Her hand moved again, toward his arm this time. He steeled himself against her touch. Her fingers closed around his wrist, loosened once, then tightened again. Beneath her fingertips, he knew his pulse was racing.

Her lips closed and the gentle rise and fall of her chest ceased. It was as though she was suddenly holding her breath, as though she had moved from dream state to consciousness. She released his wrist and her fingers drifted lower until she found his hand.

Her eyelids fluttered open, revealing eyes impossibly dark in the shadowy light.

'Andrew,' she breathed.

At the soft inflection she put on his name, his heart ceased its racing, seemed not to beat at all.

For one endless moment, her hand lay motionless in his. Her whole body was still, as though she were trying to decide. Then her forefinger drew a circle in his palm, scoring heat into his skin. A longing gripped him. He silently cursed.

With her face still soft from sleep, fine lines from a wrinkled pillow slip indented her cheek. Her eyes were soft too, although smudged with fatigue. He could see them properly now as his eyes adjusted to the lack of light, and the moon's glow coming from the window.

'You were sleeping,' he said gruffly. Ridiculous thing to say, but he was incapable of anything better.

Her eyes half closed, and without uttering a response, she raised her hand to his face and caressed the line of his jaw. His heart thumped against his chest, and his breathing grew shallow.

Unable to stop, calling himself every kind of a fool, he brought her fingers to his lips. Her scent beguiled him, pulled him, made him need her as though she were food, light and air.

She rose onto one elbow, her eyes closing further. Did she not want to see or admit to their intimacy? He traced kisses down her arm, pausing only to explore the soft hollow of its inner side.

He pushed aside her nightie's silken strap, and trailed kisses across her bare shoulder. Her skin quivered beneath his lips, and desire snaked through him. Her nipples rose against the sheerness of her nightgown, intoxicating him as the whiskey he'd drunk had not, drowning him in a torrent of need.

Stacia put her arm around his neck and pulled him close. Her lips were as he remembered, soft, but full with passion. They parted and her tongue touched his, sparking an avalanche of sensation.

He hungrily took her mouth in his, then kissed her cheek and the hollow behind her ear. Her skin was as soft as a baby's, but her body was all woman. She melted against him, her arms drawing him nearer.

He laid his head on her chest, savoring the rise of her breasts beneath his cheek and the wild thudding of her heart. Then he lifted his head and stared into her eyes. Wide open now, they stared back at his, revealing her arousal.

And her fear.

He drew away. His body stiffened, protested his brain's command. A hollow had opened within his soul begging to be filled.

But that couldn't happen. Not here. Not now. Not when the fear in Stacia's eyes jolted his suspicions into focus.

Her breasts heaved as though she'd been running, and her lips parted, gasping for air. Her fingers matched his own, curling into balls as though to stop themselves from taking all that they wanted.

'Andrew,' she said again, shakily this time.

'Don't worry,' he said, sucking in a deep breath, 'nothing is going to happen.' But nothing his brain commanded could stop his hand from touching hers. Her fingers were cold as ice.

She stared down at their locked hands, the expression in her eyes dazed.

'I'll see you in the morning,' he said, wishing the morning was now.

She opened her mouth to speak, but

in the end bit her lip. He managed, somehow, to turn and walk out the door, but the sound of her heart still beat in his head, and the scent of her perfume still clung to his clothes.

It was hours before he returned, and when he did, he listened from the doorway before entering. Stacia's breathing was slow and regular. She was asleep once more. Light from the bathroom shafted through the blackness. She'd left it on for him.

As Nancy used to do.

Andrew beat back his memories and tiptoed into the room. He moved noiselessly to the cupboard where it took only seconds to find Stacia's bag and extract the package. He carried it into the bathroom and laid it on the counter, quickly easing open the wrapping. An envelope and sweater spilled into his hands.

For a long moment, he stared down at them, then carefully re-wrapped the package. He doused the light, not wanting to see his face in the mirror, or see reflected back at him his own certainty of Stacia's involvement.

He replaced the package in her bag, then leaned his forehead for a moment against the cool metal of the cupboard door. He had promised himself to see this through to the end, and for Nancy's sake, he would, but it suddenly seemed the most difficult task in the world.

* * *

Someone had drawn the curtains. Stacia's brow creased as she stared at the offending lengths of crisp lace. They'd been open last night. The last view she remembered was the pillars of the Parthenon glowing in the distance vibrantly lit by moonlight.

Andrew. She moaned, and pressed her eyes shut. She'd come near to making the biggest mistake of her life last night, by allowing herself to forget who she was with and why. Andrew's hard lips and slow hands made her want to forget. Hands that warmed, then burned, then drove her to desire what she couldn't have. Hands compelling her to forget what she needed to remember.

She propped herself up and twitched the curtains open. The sun swept in, stinging eyes already burning from lack of sleep. But it was perfect weather for a tourist and as soon as she got rid of the package, that was what she intended to be.

Scraping her hair back from her face, she flung the covers off her legs. She'd have a shower, get dressed, and be out of this room before Andrew returned from wherever he had gone. The restaurant? The lobby? She didn't know and didn't care. Then she glanced to her right and her breath fled her lungs.

One of Andrew's long legs dangled over the arm of the sofa, while the other was bent at the knee and flopped over the side. The blanket he'd thrown over himself wasn't made to cover a man his size. It began at mid-chest and ended at his knees.

She had tried to convince herself the

desire she'd felt the night before had only been a dream, but this was no dream. Her heart pounded, her pulse hammered, and her blood raged through her veins.

A tap sounded at the door. Stacia jumped, and snatched on her dressing gown, hurrying to answer before whoever it was knocked a second time.

'A letter for Roberts,' the porter said, when she opened the door a crack and peeped through.

'That's me,' Stacia whispered.

The young man handed her a stiff white envelope, then waited with an expectant expression on his face.

'I'm sorry,' she stammered, miserably aware of her empty wallet. 'I don't have anything for you. I . . . I haven't been to the bank yet.'

'No matter, madam,' the porter said graciously.

Stacia eased the door shut. Her name was the only writing showing on the outside of the envelope. Unless the police had found her purse, no doubt empty of money and tickets, the letter had to be from Andropolous. She stuck her finger beneath the flap and ripped it open along the top. A single piece of note paper was tucked inside.

Dear Miss Roberts,

I apologize for being unable to meet you at the restaurant. Business necessitated that I leave for Crete immediately. Meet me in Agios Nikolaos on Tuesday. I will contact you at the Hotel Minos.

Andropolous

Agios Nikolaos! It would cost money to get there and she had none.

'Who was at the door?'

Stacia twisted around, jerking the note behind her back. A wide awake, standing-at-alert Andrew, faced her.

'No one,' she said.

He stared at her in disbelief.

Heat spread across her face. She tugged at the belt of her dressing gown, attempting to tighten it, succeeding only in pulling her wrap off center.

'Just the porter,' she added. With any luck, Andrew would let it go at that.

Beneath his tousled hair, Andrew's eyes narrowed. 'What did he want?'

'Someone else.' She crossed her fingers behind her back. She was getting good at this lying thing. Too good.

Andrew took a step closer.

It took all her determination to keep from retreating.

'This hotel is too expensive,' she said. 'We should check out.' Her father had once told her the best defense was a good offense. He had been referring to basketball, but the principle must be the same.

'I'll let you know when money's a problem.'

'I've been in your hair long enough.'

'If this is about last night — '

'It isn't,' she denied hastily. Maybe direct was the route to take. 'I have to go to Crete.'

'What's in Crete?'

'Minoan ruins.' She'd seen pictures

of the ruins, though she knew little else about the islands.

'There are plenty of ruins in Athens.'

'Listen,' she snapped, 'if you're worried about getting your money — '

'I'm not worried.'

'I would only need a hundred dollars or so.' The request stuck in Stacia's throat. Her grandmother had petit-pointed the maxim 'Neither a borrower nor a lender be' and had hung it in her front sitting room, where it had stared Stacia in the face every time she visited.

'If you could lend me the money, I'd be grateful,' Stacia went on hastily. 'Once I contact the Embassy, a new passport and money will arrive in no time.'

'I'll go with you.'

'No!'

'I don't mind.'

'Well, I do. I've burdened you long enough with my problems. Just lend me the money and I'll be gone.'

'That's what I'm afraid of,' Andrew said.

6

She looked lonely standing all by herself at the ship's railing. Andrew knew what it was to be lonely. Usually, he was able to ignore such feelings and throw himself into his work, his only salvation since Nancy had died. Work had been the only thing keeping guilt at bay. But this time, it was different.

He moved to stand next to her.

She eyed him warily.

'Did you get what you wanted?' he asked.

'Yes,' she answered shortly.

'Steerage?'

Her smile was faint, but it softened the barrier of her eyes. 'They call it standard.'

'Standard,' he repeated. A ridiculous category for a woman like her. 'So what does that give you? A chair in the cafeteria.'

'One on deck,' she said, shrugging.

Andrew took a deep breath, determined to keep the anger from his voice. 'There's no need for this.'

'There's every need.' She stared out at the water again, closing him out.

'Sleeping on deck isn't safe.'

Her skin pulled taut over her cheek bones. 'That's not your concern.'

She was right. Her safety should mean nothing to him. Not if she was the enemy. And if she was the enemy, why did he want her so?

Stacia took a deep breath. She couldn't afford to let Andrew see she was afraid. Her father had said animals could sense fear, and when they did, they'd go for your jugular.

No doubt Andrew would too.

'Do you plan to visit your mother while you're in Greece?' she asked, surprised her voice sounded normal.

'My mother?' he repeated, looking at her as though she was demented.

'You said she was Greek.'

'She's dead.' His eyelids half-closed,

but not before she caught a glimpse of the sadness lurking behind.

'I'm sorry,' she said softly. She knew what death was, knew it was impossible to hang on to anyone, no matter how much you needed them.

He shrugged, but his shoulders seemed stiff. 'It was a long time ago.' His lips were stiff too.

'And your father?' For a moment, Stacia didn't think he would answer.

'God knows,' he said finally, his face as dark as thunder. 'Haven't seen him in years.'

She frowned.

'He walked out on my mother and me twenty years ago, and took my older brother along for the ride.'

She could feel his pain as though it were inside her. She pressed her eyes shut and fought it the only way she knew how. The way she had fought the agony when her own mother had died, by forcing it into a small corner of her heart and ruthlessly pretending it didn't exist.

Her method didn't work any better now than it had before, and her hand stole sideways to cover his long fingers with her shorter ones. His hand rested, for an instant, under hers, so strong and hard it was impossible to believe he was capable of feeling distress. Then with a fierce glance in her direction, he snatched it away.

Stacia stared at her hand, and a numbness spread through her as she realized what Andrew had just admitted. Somehow, feeling his pain, she had missed the implications of that statement. He did have an older brother! Perhaps a brother named Andropolous, making old Mr. Andropolous, Andrew's father. What if Andropolous senior was about to hurt Andrew all over again by leaving everything to Andrew's older brother?

She shook her head. It couldn't be. It was not Andrew's father who was Greek, but his mother. Doubt crept over her. She had only Andrew's word that any of what he said was true.

'Are you hungry?' he asked.

'No,' she replied. A lump formed in her throat, impeding her breath.

'Thirsty?' he persisted.

'No,' she answered faintly. 'I want to get settled for the night.'

He touched her shoulder with his hand. 'Take my cabin,' he growled. 'I'll sleep on deck.'

'No!'

'Why are you so damned stubborn?'

'I'm not stubborn.'

'Afraid then?'

She wrenched away from his hand and faced him, seeing a strange expression in his eyes, as though he wanted her to say something, but didn't believe she would.

'I'm not afraid of anything,' she whispered.

He stepped closer.

She felt suddenly dizzy.

'I don't think that's true.'

She turned away once more, didn't dare risk the hypnotic pull of his eyes. The last of the day's light sank into the

Mediterranean like a lance thrown by Zeus. Lights sparkled in the east, twinkling like fireflies with the movement of the ship. Other people's homes, on islands she'd only dreamed about, families gathered around the table, talking . . . sharing . . . Everybody safe within the light, the darkness at bay.

She faced Andrew once more. His eyes, black in the fading light, made her mouth go dry.

'Admit it,' he insisted, 'or someday you'll wish you had.' He tilted up her chin. 'Someday you'll tell me the truth.'

'You're a fine one to talk.' She wrenched her chin from his hand. 'If anyone's been avoiding the truth, it's you.'

'What do you mean?' A warning light appeared in his eyes.

Too late, she realized she couldn't do this now, didn't want to know what he had to tell her, couldn't bear to discover he was the man she'd been warned against. Couldn't bear to find out her fears regarding him were real.

'We're both saying things we don't mean,' she said shakily. 'I suggest we go back to how it was before.'

'And how was that?' His voice seemed to come out of nowhere and everywhere, to be a series of disembodied sounds in the blackness surrounding her.

'Fellow travelers on vacation. Out to have a good time and to see the sights.'

'Is that how you want it?'

'Yes,' she said, her heart dying within.

'Then that's how it'll be.'

* * *

The wooden slats of the deck lounger dug into Stacia's spine and a film of dew glistened on the blanket pulled up around her chin. She frowned. There had been no blanket over her when she'd thrown herself onto the chair the night before, still shaking from her exchange with Andrew.

Her package. Panicky, she pushed the blanket down to her waist and felt beneath her chair.

131

Nothing.

She was unable to catch her breath, her heart pounded so frantically. Scissoring her legs, the blanket dropped to the ground beside her. Something rough scraped against the underside of her knee.

Her bag. Safe. Lodged between her legs at the foot of the lounger. She snatched it up. It seemed to weigh the same. She unclasped the catch and peered inside. Package still there. It was as if flannel surrounded her brain, blocking all her senses. Only one thing was clear. *She* had not been the one to put her bag between her legs.

'Morning,' Andrew drawled.

Stacia jerked her head in the direction of his voice. A few yards down the deck, Andrew lay sprawled on a lounger identical to her own. His face was beard-stubbled and his eyelids heavy with sleep, but the eyes behind the lids were razor sharp.

'Sleep well?' he inquired. His gaze scanned the length of her, from crumpled blanket on the deck, to clutched bag, to her doubtless frantic face.

'Did you put the blanket over me?' she demanded. And moved her bag? Had he looked in it?

'A little nippy out last night,' he said, with a shrug.

'If I needed a blanket I'd have fetched one myself.'

'Except you did need it and you didn't fetch it.'

'What are you doing here anyway? Did you sleep in that chair all night?'

'Would you rather I left you to the mercy of every low life on board?' His eyes took on fire. '*And* let your precious bag be stolen as well as your purse.'

'That wouldn't have happened.'

'You were sleeping when I checked on you. Curled up in a ball, with your back to your bag.' He snorted. 'Next time I won't bother!'

Stacia clenched her hands into fists. He was so damn protective. It was so damn irritating. And she hated like hell to admit this time he'd been right.

'Thank you,' she said finally, but spoke the words softly. Courtesy was satisfied, but maybe he wouldn't hear.

'You're welcome.'

He had heard. He suddenly grinned, his smile unexpectedly diffusing the worst of her outrage.

'Just don't do it again,' she admonished. 'I might not be so grateful the next time.'

He chuckled. The sound warmed her. It seemed days since she'd last laughed, since she'd begun this 'so-called' vacation, in fact. She couldn't prevent her own chuckle from escaping.

'Now we're friends again,' Andrew said, his laughter fading, 'where are we headed when we get off this tub?'

Friends? she thought, sobering as fast as he had. Is that what they were? How could she be friends with a man she knew so little about, wasn't sure she should trust? He could be the younger son of Mr. Andropolous, just stringing her along. Besides, no *friend* dreamed about kissing and touching the other person.

'You don't have to go anywhere with me.' If only she could forget how it felt when his lips touched hers. 'You're spoiling your own trip.'

'Not true!' His smile teased. 'I've come close to being blown to kingdom come, I've chased a purse snatcher, booked into the honeymoon suite of an expensive hotel with a beautiful young woman, chased a knife-wielding yahoo, seen the Acropolis in the moonlight — ' He spread his hands out before her. 'Traveling with you is an adventure.'

She looked at him dubiously. He made it sound as though he were enjoying himself, while she . . .

'Miss Roberts!'

Stacia swung around. 'Miss Argyle!'

The old woman shuffled along the deck toward them, clutching the rail with one hand and her cane in the other.

'Fancy meeting you again, my dear. And your young man, too.' She smiled at them both. 'Although, why I'm surprised, I can't say. I keep bumping into the same people over and over, as though the same travel agent prepared our itinerary. Very pleasant, really.' She frowned. 'Although there was that nasty young man I met in Paris who turned up in Rome, as well. I can't say I was happy to see him again! Wanted me to lend him money or some such nonsense.' She drew her shoulders back and her mouth pursed. 'For a real emergency, I wouldn't have minded, but — ' She inclined her head toward them. ' — I rather suspect he intended to buy drugs.'

'Oh,' Stacia said faintly, then collected herself. 'I didn't see you on board last night.'

Miss Argyle gestured toward the sea. 'I'm not a very good sailor. I kept to my cabin, ordered a pot of tea and a plate of dry toast, and tried to make the best of it.'

'Are you feeling better now?' Stacia asked. She glanced out past the railing toward the water. There was a faint chop on its surface.

'Not much,' Mary Argyle admitted. Her fingers tightened on the railing. 'But the steward told me we would be docking soon so I thought I would venture out.'

'Have a seat,' Andrew offered. He got to his feet and gestured to his chair.

'How kind.'

The ship suddenly rolled and the deck shifted. With a moan, Mary scuttled toward Andrew's chair. She settled there, and shut her eyes.

Stacia glanced at Andrew over the older woman's reclined form. It seemed easier all of a sudden, with Mary Argyle there, to avoid answering uncomfortable questions.

Without warning, the older woman opened her eyes. 'What part of Crete are you visiting?' she asked Stacia.

'We were just thrashing that out,' Andrew said. 'What about it, Stacia? Where to next?'

She ran her tongue over her lips and

wished the answer were simple. If she could have given Andropolous the package, she'd now be in tourist mode.

'Agios Nikolaos,' she admitted softly, trying not to sound dubious, wishing she knew exactly where it was.

'Agios Nikolaos.' Andrew regarded her thoughtfully. 'There's nothing there but a village.'

'Great beach, I understand.' She could only hope that was true, that the town wasn't in some remote mountain eyrie.

'Not particularly,' he countered.

Stacia's heart sank.

'It's a fishing village. Good harbor, small beach.'

At least it was on the coast.

'Lovely coastline outside of town,' he added. 'Plenty of hotels.'

'A friend recommended it,' Stacia said firmly. 'That's where I'm going.'

★   ★   ★

Contentment bubbled forth from Stacia's lips in a sigh. Nothing could interfere with her enjoyment of this moment, not Andrew, not the package, not Mr. Andropolous. *This* was the reason she'd come to Greece; this scenery, these people, this clarity of air.

Stacia leaned far over her hotel balcony railing. In order to see everything, she *had* to lean.

The Hotel Minos didn't face the sea, but even that was perfect. Her room overlooked an emerald lake locked behind the crowded harbor, joined to the sea by a narrow canal. Hotels and restaurants stretched to her right, while across the water and to her left rose a hill, mirrored in the lake as a smoky blue shadow.

Below, next to the water's edge, fishermen gathered in the morning sun around spindly-legged tables, drinking thick, black coffee from doll-sized cups. Knots of women in black wool shawls, bundled up in dark skirts falling below the knee, clustered outside the narrow doorways leading into the shops. Their roughly woven baskets overflowed with fruit, cheese and inexpensive wine.

Stacia heaved another happy sigh. The scene was just as she'd expected from the books she'd read, just as she had seen on the library travel videos. Only better.

She would straighten her room, then go out and explore, buy her own bread, and some pungent goat's cheese, perhaps a bottle of wine. She hugged herself in anticipation, resolutely determined to keep at bay all worries connected to the undelivered package.

There'd been no note waiting for her when she checked into the hotel, no cryptic message from Andropolous telling her to leave Agios Nikolaos and go on to the next town, the next island. So for the next few hours, at least, she planned to enjoy herself.

If only she could stop thinking about Andrew. It was one thing to put the package out of her mind, eradicating thoughts of the man was quite another! Images revolved through her brain of Andrew's hard body pressed against her own, the laughter in his sapphire eyes scattering her suspicions, and his chuckle rumbling up from his chest like water from a well, refreshing . . . sustaining.

Doubt clouded her thoughts. No matter how terrible it felt believing Andrew was the youngest Andropolous son — deep inside, when she was with him, she felt safe. A shiver skittered across her shoulders as she acknowledged the dreaded word. *Safety* had always been a delusion in the past.

A knock sounded at her door.

She cast a last, longing glance at the scene below, then hurried through the balcony doors into her room. She winced at the sight of her clothes strewn over every available surface. Her wet stockings were draped over the top of the closet door and dripped onto a folded towel below, her linen dress was flung over the wooden back of a chair, and her white cotton pants peeked from between box spring and mattress in her desperate attempt to flatten the wrinkles her borrowed travel iron couldn't smooth.

At the hotel in Athens there had been no privacy to sort through her things, to shake out her clothes and wash those made dirty from their tumble along the airport floor. But here in Agios Nikolaos, she had her own room. She had insisted on that and Andrew hadn't protested.

She had even handed him a list of what she owed him so far, everything neatly entered and tallied on a page. He had simply raised one eyebrow, folded the paper twice, then tucked it away in his wallet.

Another knock, louder this time. She swept her hand along the accordion-shaped top of the metal heating pipes and retrieved a fistful of rainbow-colored underwear. She plunged them into the voluminous pocket of her skirt and cautiously opened the door.

'Ready to go?' Andrew said, flashing a smile.

'Go where?' she asked, standing as tall as she was able, wishing she could somehow hide the chaos behind her.

'On a picnic,' he replied, holding up a basket.

Inviting scents filtered through the gaily painted handkerchief on top. Stacia lifted one end and peeked inside. *Dolmades, Feta* cheese, a jar of olives, fresh red tomatoes, and a loaf of crusty bread took up most of the space, along with a bottle of chilled white wine. Local, from the look of the printing on the label. No doubt delicious, as was everything she had tasted in Greece so far. In one corner of the basket, barely visible beneath a bunch of plump red grapes, lay two honey drenched squares of *baklava*.

She hadn't realized how hungry she was until the sight and smell of the food made her mouth water. She glanced up at Andrew and without warning was claimed by a hunger of a different sort.

'So grab your bathing suit — ' Andrew's blue gaze shifted off her and examined the room beyond.

Stacia felt a jolt of loss.

' — if you can find it.'

'I know exactly — '

'Is this — '

His fingers brushed her elbow. Before she could protest, a pair of her silk panties had been whisked from her pocket and now hung from his fingers.

'No!' She snatched the wisp of fuchsia from his hand and lay her underwear back on the heater. 'It isn't.' She took a step backwards and reached toward a pile next to her pillow. 'This is.' She held up two scarlet strips. 'Now get out of here and let me change.'

His smile deepened and, for an instant, she fancied it was approving, but he turned and left before she could tell for sure.

* * *

The sun was hotter in the open. Much hotter than in town where whitewashed buildings cast slivers of shade. Out here, there was nothing to cut the glare except the occasional tree standing alone. On the hillside beyond, an olive grove grew, the trees' leaves shimmering silver in the breeze.

Stacia streaked her hair back from her face, surprised, in the dry air, to find the strands damp against her fingers. She liked the heat, enjoyed the warmth on her toes and legs, on her fingers and arms.

Like the touch of a lover.

Heat flushed her face, and she glanced at Andrew, her body suddenly burning with a deeper heat, one she dared not examine too closely.

'We're almost there,' Andrew said. The warmth seemed to affect him, also. His hair curled damply around the edges, and his cheeks were a ruddy brown.

'Almost where?' She made herself stare past him to the sea beyond. The water enticed, seemed as cool and unattainable as a mirage.

Andrew shifted the picnic basket to his other hand and pointed. His knapsack, bulging with a blanket and two towels, traveled up his back with the movement.

'There,' he said, indicating a white-plastered, low-ceilinged building in the distance.

'What is it?'

'A villa. A hotel at the top of the season. This time of year — ' He shrugged. ' — it should be deserted.'

Deserted. Stacia's steps faltered. Where she would be alone with a man she probably shouldn't trust, a man she was starting to care about.

'You've been here before?' She hoped her question would cover the sudden thumping of her heart and tightness in her throat.

'Once,' he said, his voice distant. His eyes, when she ventured another look, seemed to be focussed inward to some other time.

Slowly, she moved toward the villa, not asking any more questions.

The closer they got, the larger the building loomed. It turned out not to be a single building at all, but separate structures attached by covered walk-ways. In the morning sun, the red tile roofs were bright against the white walls, the blue sea visible through the walkways.

Andrew stopped all of a sudden and Stacia stopped, too, entranced by the villa's charm. Unexpectedly, he took her hand. It felt good, as though hand in hand was the only way they could enter such a magical place.

'This way,' Andrew said.

Stacia followed him beneath a late blooming orange tree. The tangy bouquet of its blossoms tickled her nose and followed her into the passageway, where it lingered around her as they walked.

It was cool beneath the red tile roof. A relief after the heat. Even so, her breathing had become irregular and shallow, and some emotion of Andrew's had transmitted itself to her. Perhaps it was the way he held himself so stiffly that made her apprehensive, for she suddenly longed to stay where they were, safe in the cool darkness, out of the light.

Incomprehensibly, Andrew moved faster, pulling her along with him. As swiftly as they had entered the passage, they were suddenly out again. Stacia blinked as the glare bombarded her eyes before settling into shape and form.

The villa was not one level as she had thought, but rather three. Large shady rooms were sunk deep into the cliff face high above the sea, like the mountain top aeries of eagles. A single balcony stretched the length of each level, its marble floor showing up blue-veined against the darker rock of the cliff. A railing of wood and plaster rose chest high, tall enough to lean and dream against.

Flowers, as profuse in quantity as they were in variety, grew up from red clay pots, well placed to catch whatever rainwater fell. Flowering vines twined up the posts of the balcony and along the lattice-work at the top.

Stacia let go of Andrew's hand, felt the

loss of the connection the moment she had done so. She walked swiftly to the railing and looked over, praying the hair falling around her face would cover her confusion. The railing's plaster was cool against her arms, welcomingly, blissfully, cool.

The levels below were identical to the one they were on; all cunningly cut into the cliff side, all fronted by a flower-filled balcony, and all joined one to the other by a twisting marble staircase.

But it was the sea that drew Stacia's eye, stretching before her in shimmering variations of aquamarine, turquoise and green, the color changing with the water's depth and the way the sun struck its surface.

'Beautiful,' Andrew said, his hands appearing next to hers on the railing.

Taking in a deep breath, Stacia faced him. A smile spread slowly across his lips and she went weak at the knees.

He gazed at her for one endless, breathless moment, until such a pressure built within her chest, she felt she might explode from its exquisite agony. Then his gaze shifted and moved beyond, seemed to encompass everything at once; the balconies, the sea, even the rocks below.

'Seems smaller,' he murmured.

'Smaller?' Stacia asked. 'What is?'

'Everything.' Again he bathed her with his smile.

'When were you last here?' She knew she had to ask, but was unable to halt the constriction of her heart.

'When I was five.' His lips drooped ruefully at the corners. 'That explains it, I suppose.'

She forced herself to smile back, forced herself to relax. 'Everything seems enormous when you're little,' she agreed. Her grandmother Roberts' house had seemed cavernous and terrifying. It wasn't until she was older that the building shrunk to a normal size.

'Were you here with your mother's family?' Stacia's heart beat faster.

Andrew's eyes softened. 'No. Just my mother, father and brother.'

This was the moment she'd both anticipated and dreaded. The moment he told her who he was and what he wanted. She glanced wildly around, first at the sea then at the flowers, hoping somehow their normality would keep her worst fear at bay — that he was after the will.

People killed for money.

Sweat beaded her forehead and rolled down her temples, the world seeming suddenly filled with silence, a particularly loud and terrifying silence. She could no longer hear the drone of the honey bees hovering over the scarlet petals of the hibiscus. The lap of the waves onto the rocks below became muted. The only sound penetrating her consciousness was the thump of her own heart battering against her chest.

'It was fabulous,' Andrew added, when finally, inevitably, his eyes focussed on hers. He swallowed hard. 'The last good time we had together.' The animation in his face disappeared, leaving a flatness on his features.

And in Stacia's heart.

She knew all about *last times*. Before her mother died . . . With a shudder, Stacia jerked herself free of memories. This wasn't about her mother, or her father, either. This was about Andrew, an unexpectedly vulnerable Andrew, of whom she still knew virtually nothing.

'I — '

He turned to her again, cut off her words and the sympathy she knew must be in her eyes. His smile blazed down upon her, burning her with its heat.

'It *was* a very good time.' He reached out and touched a chalky-blue flower on a trailing vine. His hand seemed enormous, the flower incredibly fragile, but his touch was so gentle the petal fluttered back into place. 'A *magical* time.' His eyes were bluer than she'd seen them before, so blue the flower looked white by comparison.

He brought his fingers to her cheek and rested them against her skin. Every nerve-ending in her body was centered on his touch. Vaguely, she was aware of a butterfly fluttering overhead and one settling on the flower next to her hand, but a fairy sprinkling magic powder couldn't have torn her attention from the man at her side.

His eyes told her that she was magic, too.

'I'm glad to be back — ' He cupped her chin in his hand. ' — this time with you.'

He was going to kiss her again. She could see it in his eyes, and in the tension of the muscles along his jaw. If he kissed her now, she would kiss him back, for he had warmed her heart and brought her soul to life. The possibility he was the enemy seemed meaningless compared to that.

But that was her heart speaking.

Her only salvation lay in listening to her head.

She drew back a fraction of an inch, and mustered all the strength she possessed not to raise her lips to his.

His eyes clouded over and he, too, pulled away. 'I almost forgot — '

His words were all but lost in the buzzing in her head.

' — friends. Fellow tourists.' A pulse throbbed at the base of his neck, and his hand dropped to his side. 'Probably better that way.' He took her hand again, held it impersonally this time.

Perversely, the pain *that* caused was more terrible than fear.

He stared down at her fingers with a wrinkled brow, as though he didn't know to whom her hand belonged. Then he glanced along the balcony and his frown deepened.

'There used to be a trail down to the sea.' His gaze returned to hers. 'Shall we go?' he challenged.

7

Stacia tried to pretend she felt nothing, but no matter how hard she tried, she couldn't breathe for the lump in her throat.

She moved carefully as she followed Andrew through a narrow archway and out onto the stone steps leading to the rocks below. She didn't want to fall, didn't want there to be a reason for Andrew to hold her again in his arms.

A huge boulder stood at the foot of the steps, a monolith standing guard to the paradise beyond. With a faint smile, Andrew edged around the rock to the right and led her along with him.

The path was little more than a goat's trail. Stacia held tightly to Andrew's hand and pressed her free hand against the rock, gripping its smooth surface as best she could.

Once around the corner, Andrew

halted so abruptly she almost trod on his heels. She stood on her tiptoes and peered over his shoulder.

A boulder lay ahead, as large as a small patio and perfectly flat. The sea lapped at its edges on two sides, occasionally throwing up spurts of water which dried the instant the liquid touched the surface of the warm rock. The large boulders formed a rock wall on the other two sides, sheltering the flat area from the wind.

It was as if this private place had been put there for their pleasure alone.

She stared suspiciously at Andrew, but from the expression on his face, he was as surprised as she. She turned quickly away again, before the danger-ous warmth flooding her body showed in her eyes as well.

'Magic,' Andrew asserted. He placed his hands on her shoulders and gently pulled her back around. 'Now do you believe in it?'

'Yes,' she whispered. Staring into his eyes she could believe in anything.

He leaned forward, and this time his lips, warm from the sunshine and salty like the sea, brushed against hers. Her own lips parted, her defenses melting.

'Friends?' he asked softly. His eyes searched hers, the word he spoke a mockery given the desire rampaging through her.

'Friends,' she said, all but choking on the word. She didn't dare tell him it wasn't enough. She didn't dare tell him anything at all. He drew away again, leaving her tingling, but alone.

How could he so easily turn away, take the blanket from his knapsack and lay it on the rock? How could he kiss her as he had and not want more? She rubbed her hand down her arm to prevent herself from reaching out to him. How could they be friends?

'Let's swim first,' Andrew said cheerfully. He dropped the picnic basket in a shady crevice beneath an outcrop of rock, then unpacked the bottle of wine and lay it in a cool pool of water captured between two rocks.

'Yes,' she agreed. Perspiration trickled uncomfortably between her breasts. She needed to cool down.

The sea, an incredible indigo in the high noon sun, was so clear Stacia could see the bottom. It appeared shallow, but given the size of the rocks lining the shore and clearly visible both above and below the water, it must be well over her head.

Andrew suddenly stripped off his shirt, exposing his muscular chest. But when he tugged down the zipper on his shorts and revealed a tight black swim suit underneath, Stacia flushed and turned away.

With trembling fingers, she unbuttoned her blouse and slipped out of it. She felt vulnerable and exposed in her bathing suit, not the experienced traveler she'd had visions of becoming.

When she glanced back toward the villa, she was astounded to discover she couldn't see it at all. The boulder marking the entrance to the flat rock blocked her view, and at the same time guarded them from the sight of any onlooker above.

They were truly alone.

Stacia's pulse raced.

She slipped out of her shorts, conscious that Andrew, who stood on the edge of the rock ready to dive into the sheltered cove, was watching her as closely as she had him. He held out his hand.

'Coming?' he asked. His eyes reflected the light bouncing off the water.

With a nod, she took hold of his hand.

They dove together, plunging deep, then deeper yet into the welcoming silky coolness of the Mediterranean sea. It wasn't until Stacia's fingertips met the fine sand on the sea's floor, that Andrew's kick thrust them back toward the surface. She moved her own feet slowly, convinced she could stay below the surface for hours if only she tried, suddenly wanting to do just that.

It was so peaceful down there, so silent. No pressure to think, to decide, or even to feel. With her eyes shut against the sting of the salt water, no weakness could invade her body with one glance from Andrew's deep blue eyes, and no pangs could pierce her heart when he spoke.

With a splutter, she broke the surface of the sea, her lungs ready to burst from lack of air. Andrew pulled her to him, his eyes filled with concern.

'I'm fine,' she choked out, but with his hands around her waist, she felt anything but fine.

Beads of water dropped from his hair to his face and shoulders, each drop a prism in the overhead sun. They blinded and confused her.

Her legs drifted between his and she kicked her feet furiously, perversely coming up hard against him instead. One touch of his body told her he had reacted to her nearness as much as she had to his. Cool water might separate them, but the distance between them closed to nothing.

The length of his body stretched

along hers, his torso lean and muscular, his hips taut. He caressed her back, fanning heat to flame.

Stacia gazed into his eyes and as suddenly as the wind dies after a storm, she no longer wanted to escape. Gripped by desire, she raised her lips to his.

He tasted of the sea and sunshine and exhilarating male. She met the hunger of his mouth with a rush of passion, wanting more than his lips and the touch of his hands. She twined her arms around his neck and pulled him nearer, choking as the sun-warmed water closed over them both.

With a powerful kick, Andrew propelled them back to the surface. With a gasp, she shook the water from her eyes.

'Kissing you can be dangerous,' Andrew murmured hoarsely.

Breathless, she pushed him away again.

'Just friends?' he asked. His eyes told her how crazy he thought that particular pretense was.

She stroked toward the flat rock. If she was to resist the lure of his eyes and body, she had to keep moving.

'Lunch,' she said, in a voice as firm as possible, thinking that if she spoke more she might break the spell.

He caught up to her and swept past, found the footholds in the rocks before she did and pulled himself out. He turned and offered his hand, but she got out herself, trying not to look in his direction.

She raised her face to the sun instead, and prayed its brilliance would hide the flush heating her cheeks.

A warm, fluffy towel dropped over her shoulders.

'I hate to cover you up,' Andrew said, 'but you mustn't catch cold.' He ran his hands down her arms.

His touch drew fire, making her understand it wasn't the cold causing her to tremble, but the heat that flowed from his body to hers.

'Lunch,' she repeated, the word more an entreaty than a suggestion.

'Soon.' He stepped in front of her, his eyes darkening to the color of the sea at midnight. 'Later,' he amended. He stared at her hungrily, as though she stood before him naked.

She knew she should protest, should insist they stop tantalizing each other with what could never be, but the words wouldn't come.

He slowly leaned toward her, so slowly a drop of water rolled down his temple and was caught in the blue-black shadow of his chin. As though she were a puppet in the hands of a master, she met his lips with hers.

His kiss stole her breath.

He explored her mouth, softly, at first, then with increasing urgency. She held herself stiffly, knowing if she reached for him, she'd be lost.

She shut her eyes. Surely nothing this wonderful could be wrong. Slowly, dazedly, she opened them again, and slid toward passion on the wings of enchantment.

His eyelashes brushed her cheek as he nuzzled his way to her hairline.

Something within exploded, too powerful to ignore and too wonderful to wish away.

The distance between them closed and the hairs on her arms rose as though reaching for him.

He pulled her closer, stroking her back in a long caressing sweep. Her skin on fire, her body melted against his harder edges. His fingers slid beneath the edge of the towel and unhooked her bikini top.

Uncountable nerve-endings blasted their message to her head and heart. From both the response was immediate. She wanted him, needed him, no matter who he was or what he was. She wanted to lie with him here under the Mediterranean sun and feel his hands on her breasts and along her body, wanted danger, and excitement, and an end to all safety.

She moaned and the sound seemed to intensify Andrew's passion. He pulled her bikini straps away from her shoulders and slid them down her arms. Then catching her to him, his hands cradled her bottom. Her nipples hardened, then squashed flat against his chest. His pelvis thrust against hers, filling her with fire.

His lips traveled across her temple to the pulse below her ear, trailing a line of heat. He gently nibbled her ear lobe, the soft pain stoking her desire. She arched against him, wanting him closer, needing him to be a part of her.

With a groan, he rained kisses down her neck to the base of her throat. At the swelling of her breasts, he lifted his head and stared deep into her eyes. He seemed to be giving her the final choice, seemed to demand she meet his lovemaking with desire of her own.

With a smile she kissed the line of his jaw, giving him her answer with her lips.

He cupped her breasts with his hands and pressed them to his mouth, stroking her inflamed and hardened nipples with his tongue. Then he swept her into his arms and deposited her gently on the sun warmed blanket. He lowered himself beside her, his body blocking the sun. But the heat blazing through her did not diminish. It came from him and from her, from both of them together, a furnace of fiery flesh and desire.

Her breath, when it came, erupted in short gasps. She was not even certain she was breathing at all. Andrew breathed for her, his mouth covering her lips as his length did her body, pinning her to the ground. But she was a willing prisoner, one whose only punishment would be his departure.

He placed one hand beneath her head, cradling and protecting her from the ground. The rock on which she lay should have been hard, but its hollow contoured her curves, provided the most natural of mattresses.

Andrew lingeringly explored her body from her breasts to her belly, then moved to the scrap of cloth lying wetly between them. He eased her bikini bottoms over her hips, then down her legs and off.

Weak with need, she ran her fingers around the waistband of his swimming trunks. His skin was warm velvet, but the hard muscles beneath snagged her breath in her throat. She tugged at his trunks, and with urgency, he helped her.

He rose above her, the sun splitting around either side of his face. His eyes were soft with want but his lips were firm and sensual. Reaching for his shorts, he extracted a packet from its pocket. She closed her eyes and felt his body shift as he slid on protection. She curved up and he thrust down, easing into her with caring and skill. A searing heat spread through her loins and he thrust faster.

He was in her, and on her, through her, and around her. Everywhere she was, he was, too. Partners in ecstacy, equals in love.

For one long shuddering moment, she heard only the sound of his passion and her own answering cry. She shut her eyes, but couldn't shut out the light.

It penetrated her consciousness as he penetrated her body, lit her from without, as he lit her from within. Burned into her fears, and dismissed them with disdain.

A wave slapped the rock not far from her head, and somewhere on the cliff side, bees buzzed over flowers. But here on the rock, none of that mattered. Andrew's passion was her passion, her joy, his. In a crescendo of sound they met and joined, then blazed together in an explosion of sensation.

For a long moment afterward he didn't move. Simply stayed where he was, his weight warm and welcome. His head rested on her chest, and he languorously curled his tongue around one nipple, teasing and enticing it, encouraging it again to tautness.

She chuckled with pleasure, a low, throaty sound she was unused to hearing from her own throat. But she was just as unused to feeling like this, as contented as a cat in sunshine, as satiated as a kitten with a belly full of cream. Joy bubbled up as though from a spring, filling her with effervescence. An unfamiliar sensation, but one she liked.

He covered her mouth with his and kissed her again, not urgently this time, but slowly as though he savored her taste.

'Friends?' he whispered, kissing his way up her cheek to her eyes.

She shut her eyes and shivered, relishing the touch of his lips on her eyelids and the feel of his manhood stirring within.

'More than that,' she whispered back, afraid to say the word lover, as though even now the magic might end. Moving her hands across his back, she found his skin slick with passion. His eyes closed and she moved to meet him once again as he thrust into her body with a rhythm as old as time.

He seemed to know instinctively what gave her pleasure, and she was stunned that two virtual strangers, two *friends*, two lovers, could produce such ecstacy.

She loved him, she suddenly realized,

with her body, soul, and mind, but most frightening of all, she loved him with her heart.

She stared into his face, memorized each plane and line, held dear the tiny scar marring his jaw.

Everything was perfect. This moment. This man. This feeling of love.

8

Andrew stared down at her, the passion in his eyes giving way to concern. His eyes grew darker and darker, as though one idea after another tumbled through his brain and not one of them had anything to do with love. He rolled off her and to his side, facing her, but apart.

'What is it?' she whispered. Joy spiralled away like water down a drain, dread filling the emptiness left behind.

He ran his finger down her throat to her breast, then, as though forcing himself, he pulled his hand away.

Aching with loss, she pulled her discarded towel across her chest. The sun still blistered down, but she suddenly felt cold. For all the sun's fiery touch, it couldn't penetrate the ice forming around her heart.

Andrew stared at his hand, the one

that had touched her, then into her eyes, his expression deadly serious.

'Perhaps — ' He paused, as though to choose his words carefully. ' — remaining friends was better.'

No, her heart protested, but she trapped the word with her lips.

'We're lovers now,' he said.

The word 'lovers' held no warmth, though the magic of their lovemaking still hung in the air around them. Involuntarily, the muscles in her pelvis contracted.

'It's time you told me the truth,' he said, his voice emotionless. He seemed to hold himself in, as if reserving judgement in some way.

Relief trickled through her. He didn't find it easy to speak the words of love. She didn't either. Wasn't it enough that they felt the love? Did either of them have to admit it out loud?

Loving wasn't safe. Admitting it wasn't safe. Love could be lost, and she'd lost enough.

She stared into his eyes, and searched

for strength, needed his assurance to say the words.

Andrew suddenly rose to a sitting position.

She struggled to her elbows, then sat up, also. Eyeball to eyeball. That was the only way she'd find the power to face him head on. She met his eyes and her heart quailed. It would take all the strength she possessed just to hold her own.

Andrew looked past her across the sunlit cove toward Agios Nikolaos. Then his lips tightened and he turned to her again. 'What's in the package, Stacia?'

Her breathing died to a shallow gasp. Obviously making love to her had meant nothing to him. While she'd been struggling to admit her love, he was thinking about something else entirely. His father's will?

She'd been a fool to think she could trust this man, a fool to ignore her own suspicions. In the end, as in the beginning, it all came down to the package.

It was as though they had never made love at all, as though she peered through tinted glasses into the darkest corner of the ocean. The sunlit cove seemed suddenly shadowed, the welcoming rocks, hard and bumpy, the food in the picnic basket, foreign and tasteless, the blanket on which they lay . . . No. No more.

Andrew was right about one thing. It was time she knew the truth.

His eyes had hardened into slate-blue orbs, eyes of a prosecutor and judge all rolled into one. From the look on his face, the decision he'd rendered was guilty.

'What's the package got to do with you?' she demanded softly, swallowing the bile rising in her throat.

He rose to his feet, his movements fluid. *Her* body felt battered and sore, as if her bones were all broken and her flesh bruised. Continuing to sit was suddenly as untenable as remaining without clothes, but her right leg buckled beneath her as she rose. She staggered against an outjutting promontory on the rocky wall. Tears filled her eyes, threatened to spill over.

He took hold of her shoulder as if to steady her, and a trembling began that buffeted her body. With a forceful shrug, she pulled herself free.

'I want to get dressed,' she said firmly. If she was going to hear his answer, she needed the armor of clothing.

His hands dropped to his sides, clenched once, then hung still, the effort of that stillness evident on his face.

She yanked on her shorts, ignoring the panties she'd packed in her bag. She would be exposed for the time it took to put them on. She'd already given him her body. Now she wanted it back.

She turned her back to him and reached for her brassiere, fumbling with the clasps as though she were a novice. She couldn't bear to look at him and see in his eyes that he'd only made love to her to get the will. Then his hand touched hers and she froze to the spot.

'Let me help,' he offered quietly, as

though he hadn't spoken earlier, as though his question no longer reverberated in her ears.

'I can do it,' she said sharply.

His hand dropped away.

Irrationally, that loss was harder to bear than his touch.

She slipped her arms through her blouse, buttoned it and faced him. His shorts were already on, but his chest was still bare. With sandals and a lance, he could be Jason arriving on Crete for the golden fleece. He seemed the personification of good standing before her, not of evil.

She cleared her throat, prayed the words she needed would come. 'You haven't answered my question.' She lifted her chin higher.

'You've got something of mine in that package,' he said, his voice suddenly hard.

Everything about him was now hard, except for the hair curling softly around his face. Yet he stared at her as though memorizing her features.

'I was warned about you,' she said.

'You know about me?' Something painful flickered across his face. 'Warned I would want my property?'

'Warned you might try to steal it.' If she said the words aloud, it might make it all seem real. Very real and very horrible. She backed away one step toward the stairs.

'Me steal it?' he asked incredulously. He took a step toward her, his gaze fastened on hers. 'They don't call it stealing when you take back what's yours.'

His gaze pinned her to the rock. She was unable to move backward, didn't want to move forward.

'Who are you?' she whispered. She needed to hear the truth, knew suddenly it was the only way to make the pain end.

'I told you who I am.'

'You gave me a name. That doesn't mean you told me the truth.'

'Why don't *you* tell *me* the truth?' His eyes were bullets, hard as metal and steely blue. 'What's in the package,

Stacia.' He gripped her wrist. 'Do you know?'

'Yes,' she breathed, bracing herself, though for what she didn't know. The completeness of their isolation, so desirable before, seemed suddenly menacing. She caught her breath and held it. He would hardly attack her. He knew she didn't have the package with her.

A sound as soft as a sigh escaped his lips. 'You're part of it, aren't you?' His fingers became an iron band around her wrist, and his eyes grew darker, though with pain or elation, she wasn't sure which. There were lines around his lips that hadn't been there before, lines scored so deep, their ridges swept down his face.

'Part of what?'

'The conspiracy,' he said, in a leaden voice. 'You knew what was in the package, yet you agreed to carry it to Greece.'

'Yes.'

He released her wrist and gripped her chin instead, tilting it upward, his eyes searching hers. Her soul too, for all she knew. Heat scored her cheeks where his fingers lay, reviving past unwanted heat.

'I didn't want to believe you knew,' he said in a contemptuous voice.

She wrenched her head away. Somehow his contempt hurt more than the knowledge he wasn't who he pretended to be.

'I'd begun to believe you were incapable of such a thing.'

'I'd do it again in an instant.' Anger added an edge to her words.

'You'll never do it again to *me*.'

The steely certainty in his voice made her want to lash out at him. 'We're *lovers* now. You said so.' She heard the bitterness in her voice and struggled to keep her feelings from her face. She had given him too much already.

'Lovers never lie,' she added softly. 'I know you're not Andrew Moore. At least, that's not your father's name.' The words tumbled from her mouth, but if she didn't speak them quickly, she might not speak them at all.

'You told me your father left when you were young, taking your brother with him.' She stared hard into his eyes. 'Your father is Andropolous, isn't he?'

Stunned surprise crossed his face.

'You found your father,' she accused, 'and planned your revenge.'

'Revenge?' he repeated.

Even as she'd said it, it sounded ridiculous. The man to whom she'd just made love wasn't capable of revenge, no matter whose son he was. Not if it meant hurting her. And hurting her was the only way he was going to get that package.

Her heartbeat faltered. Perhaps she had simply assumed he cared. *What if he hadn't?* Her palms turned clammy and fear trickled up her spine.

It was as if her eyes were open at last, looking at the truth and recoiling.

'You've been following me,' she accused. She scarcely breathed, yet every breath hurt.

'Yes,' he admitted.

'Talking to me, helping me, lending

me money.' As she ran through the list, she could feel him mentally ticking each item off.

'I talked to you because I wanted to, helped you because you needed it, lent you money for the same reason.' His voice was low and even, not a criminal's voice at all. If this were the movies he'd be shouting and waving a gun.

'You waited and watched. You took your time. You enjoyed yourself.' Her last words were as high and thin as a sorcerer's rope.

'I enjoyed being with you.' He gave her a faint smile. 'Though you aren't the easiest person alive.'

'Why didn't you just take the package?' Blood raced through her veins and hit her head. 'Why did you have to humiliate me first?'

He took another step toward her. 'I did nothing to harm you. You did that yourself.'

She could see him as clearly now as when they'd made love, but this time his lips weren't swollen with passion, nor were his eyes bright with desire. His lips were compressed now, his eyes accusing. He seemed larger, stronger, more powerful than ever.

He held her gaze with his, his eyes forcing her to stay put when reason demanded she bolt up those stairs and never look back.

'Why did you do it?' he demanded.

'It was a job like any other.'

'Not quite like any other.' A muscle along his jaw line jerked.

'Travel. Good money.' She faced him squarely. 'Hard to turn down.'

'I didn't want to believe you'd do anything for money.' His lips twisted. 'I guess I was wrong.'

She shook her head in dismissal, her stomach churning with the knowledge that even now she knew the truth about him, she cared what he thought.

'Why chase half way across the world after me?' she asked.

'You have what I want.'

'You should have talked to your father?'

'I have no father.'

'He'd have treated you fairly.'

'Alive, or dead, he never treated anyone fairly. But what's that got to do with this.' The crease in his forehead deepened.

She resisted the urge to smooth it away. 'He's old and confused.' No more confused than she.

'Who is?' he demanded.

'Mr. Andropolous,' she said impatiently. The perplexed look on Andrew's face made her long to shake him. 'Your *father.*'

'My father?' he repeated stupidly.

'Stop it,' she commanded. She couldn't look at him and discuss this, all the while wanting him. Look at him and know he didn't really want her.

He gripped her shoulders. 'My father's dead,' he said again.

'Then . . . who is Andropolous?' Her head was swirling. The pieces of the puzzle shifted like sand on a desert.

'Exactly,' he said icily. 'Who is Andropolous?'

'Mr. Stone's client,' she explained, then was instantly furious she had done so. She owed him nothing.

'Mr. Stone?' he demanded sharply.

'The man who hired me.'

'Wilson.'

A chill streaked down her arms at the ice in his voice.

'Stone,' she insisted. 'He said his name was Stone.'

'And you believed him.'

'Yes,' she whispered. 'I believed what he told me.' Though obviously, she was no judge of what was true, or who to believe. An emptiness grew inside her, a desolation of spirit telling her nothing he could say mattered.

'Stacia.' He shook her shoulders, as though what he was about to ask mattered more than anything on earth. 'What do *you* think is in the package?'

She hesitated and was lost. There was no point in prevaricating if he was telling the truth about his father being dead.

'Mr. Andropolous's last will and

testament.' Hope flickered at the confused expression on Andrew's face. If he wasn't Andropolous's son, he wasn't the villain she'd been warned against.

'There was more than paper in that package,' Andrew said tersely. His fingers tightened as if by reflex.

'Just a sweater.' She reached up and grabbed his wrists, unprepared for the current jolting through her when they touched. She snatched away her hands, sure they'd been burned.

His eyes seemed on fire, also. Their indigo color darkened, settled finally at black, but within their depths, a light flashed.

'How do you know it's a sweater?' he asked, his voice low and accusing.

'I opened it,' she said, flushing.

He released her so abruptly she felt disconnected. 'Come on,' he ordered. He snatched up the food basket and blanket. The light in his eyes burned brighter than ever. 'Let's look at it together.'

Andrew had set the pace of a marathon runner, racing back to the hotel with one hand gripping her elbow as though she were a prisoner. Though chilled with apprehension, her skin was slick with sweat, and the sun seemed as determined to blind her as Andrew was to rush her. She stumbled once, but that barely slowed him. He held her weight and pulled her on her way again.

She peered at the key in her hand, her eyes still adjusting to the comparative darkness of the hall. She felt for the key hole and inserted it into the lock. A click, a grating of tumblers, and suddenly they were through.

She took in a deep breath and surveyed her room slowly, aware of Andrew at her back, aware of his impatience. The room seemed unfamiliar, as though it had changed in the hours she'd been gone, but perhaps it was she who had done the changing. She ran her tongue around the inside of her mouth and across her lips, the only dry parts of her body.

'Get the package,' Andrew demanded.

Slowly, reluctantly, she moved toward her suitcase, opened it in front of him and took out the parcel. She faced him and found that even now he moved her, standing before her as he did, tall, strong and handsome. What struck her most was the clarity of his eyes.

Honest eyes, she would have thought.

'Open it,' he ordered.

She lifted her chin. 'I'm opening nothing. Not until you tell me your interest in this.'

Too swiftly for her to stop him, he stepped closer and snatched the package. Only then did he look at her.

His eyes were the blue of the Mediterranean sky. Clear eyes. Open. Eyes you could trust.

She dropped her gaze and stared at his hands instead. She'd come close to trusting him once. That wouldn't happen again.

'My name is Andrew Moore,' he told her for a second time. 'What's in the package is mine.'

His words were clear enough, but it wasn't his words that worked on her doubts. It was his voice. The firm, certain voice of someone who is sure.

She gazed numbly up at him.

'Open it,' he said, holding the package toward her.

She couldn't do what he said. Not in front of him. Her breathing slowed, her heart thudded, then slowly, reluctantly, she put out her hand.

It felt as it always did. The same weight, the same soft solidity, the faint crinkle of paper when squeezed.

'It's not yours to see,' she protested, staring once more into his eyes.

'What's in the package is mine and I'm telling you to open it.'

If she didn't open it, he would. Stacia started at a corner, gently eased the tape from the paper. She was torn between making sure the contents of the package could be put back no one the wiser, and ripping it open and flinging it in Andrew's face.

The sweater spilled into her hands.

Black, the color of Greece, of dignity, and wisdom.

Stacia lowered her gaze to cover her anguish. She had known what was in the package, but had prayed that somehow a miracle would occur, that the contents would become what Andrew expected.

He took the sweater from her hand and held it by its shoulders. An envelope fell to the floor between them. There was no avoiding his eyes now. Bleakly, she looked up.

He wasn't looking at her, but was staring grimly at the sweater. When he did look up, a line scored his brow.

'You didn't know, did you?' His voice resonated with relief.

'Know what?' she asked, her voice dull with sorrow. 'That you weren't telling me the truth?'

9

A knock sounded at the door, lightly, at first, with the knuckles, then harder, as though whoever it was had stretched their fingers flat and now pounded with their palms.

With difficulty Stacia wrenched her gaze off Andrew, but was unable to lift the numbness in her soul, unable to respond to the message her brain sent demanding movement.

Andrew dropped the sweater onto Stacia's bed and answered the door for her. He flung it wide, then stood aside so Stacia could see.

'Miss Argyle!' Stacia whispered, her voice deadened with the pain still lapping at her heart.

'Thank heavens, it *is* you.' Mary Argyle stepped inside, her face grey beneath the dusting of make-up she'd applied to her dry skin. Lines ran between her brows and her chest heaved.

'Are you all right?' Stacia asked. Impulsively, she clasped the older woman's hand, whose fingers felt as fragile as the bones of a bird.

'No. Yes. I . . . I think so,' Mary said uncertainly. Her gaze darted from Stacia to Andrew, then lit back on Stacia.

'You're ice cold,' Stacia exclaimed. She gently massaged the older woman's hand, just as she had massaged her grandmother's limbs when the winter weather brought on her arthritis. But it wasn't cold here. Sweat trickled down Stacia's spine, gluing her cotton blouse to her back.

'Thank goodness you're here,' Mary fluttered again. 'I spotted you this morning from my balcony. I had no idea we'd booked into the same hotel. I asked the clerk — ' She panted for air as though she were all out.

'What's happened?' Andrew demanded.

The old woman's hand suddenly clenched, squeezing Stacia's fingers with surprising strength.

'No doubt, I'm being foolish,' Mary said, her voice wavering. 'Someone tried to get into my room.'

'Break in, you mean?' Stacia cried.

'Just a moment ago.' Mary's blue eyes watered. 'I don't know if he's still around or not, but he frightened me.'

'Which room is yours,' Andrew demanded.

'Just down the hall from this one. Number 416.'

Andrew strode through the door and into the hall.

'You mustn't go after him yourself,' Mary called out, but Andrew had already disappeared. She took a small step forward, as though she meant to follow. 'It's dangerous,' she finished feebly, teetering back onto her heels. She sank onto Stacia's bed.

Stacia watched her worriedly.

'Your young man might get hurt,' the older woman said.

'He's not my young man,' Stacia protested automatically, but her protest was no longer truthful and that scared her more than any possible thief lurking about. It was dangerous to allow herself to care this much, to love Andrew, and need him, to want him to need her.

Mary gazed skeptically at her.

'He won't get hurt,' Stacia said fiercely, wishing she could be sure of that. She wanted Andrew to walk safely through the doorway this minute.

With a sudden shiver, Mary clasped together her trembling hands. 'I hope so, my dear. I hope so.'

'You're cold,' Stacia said, sitting next to her on the bed. Her own teeth began to chatter.

'Perhaps just a little.' Mary picked up Mr. Andropolous's sweater. 'Might I just wrap this around my — '

'No!'

At Stacia's exclamation, Mary's eyes filled with astonishment.

Stacia swallowed hard and held out her hand. 'It's not my sweater,' she said more quietly.

'I thought you might have made it,'

Mary said, with a faint smile. 'I knit myself, you know. Nothing so lovely or ambitious as this. Just baby sweaters and the like for my nephew's children.' She rubbed her hand over the wool. 'But this is new. Did Andrew give it to you?' She didn't wait for Stacia to respond, didn't look at her even. Mary's gaze was on the wool, her fingers gently caressing. 'I'm sure he didn't mean anything untoward by it, dear,' she continued on primly. 'It's a lovely souvenir from Crete.'

'I — '

'Although you can never be sure, can you?' Two spots of pink formed on the older woman's cheeks. Her eyes grew brighter, too. 'In my day, no woman would consider accepting a present from a young man, excepting, of course, if they were engaged.' She stared curiously at Stacia. 'Are you engaged, my dear?'

'No,' Stacia said firmly, and got to her feet.

'But something has happened. Your

face is quite flushed.'

Nothing had happened. Nothing with any meaning. If she said it often enough, perhaps she would believe it. Making love had meant nothing to Andrew, and to survive she had to convince herself it meant nothing to her either.

'You don't have to tell me,' Mary said briskly. 'Perhaps it's the sort of news you'll want to share with your mother first.'

Her mother. Stacia's throat closed over. Her mother had missed most of her other firsts: her first day at high school, her first piano recital, her first date, the first time she'd made love . . . Stacia averted her head, tears rolling down her cheeks. It wasn't her mother's fault. She had wanted to live, not die.

The old woman touched her shoulder with a trembling hand. Stacia drew in a deep breath, and swiftly swept away her tears.

'There's nothing to tell,' she said numbly. She had to start now as she meant to go on — strongly, independently. Yet she was caught in her doubts and the icy grip of fear.

Mary's gaze jerked toward the balcony. 'Did you hear something?' she asked hoarsely. She moved toward the sliding door and opened it.

'When?' Stacia whispered.

'Just now. A noise.' The old woman clutched the black sweater to her chest. 'Outside, I think.'

'Impossible,' Stacia said, her heart beginning to race. 'We're four stories up.' But she had no intention of venturing out onto that balcony, or allowing Mary to go there either. Dark was beginning to fall, and if a thief did roam the building, she didn't want to meet him.

'It's possible to climb from balcony to balcony,' Mary said fearfully.

'Surely not!'

'Two years ago, in Egypt, I had a thief in my room.' The old woman turned toward the balcony doors. 'The balcony ran the length of the building.

He jimmied my door open.' She gave a delicate shudder. 'Since then, I've been very careful.'

'How do you mean?'

Mary's bird face turned pink. 'My nephew made me a wedge of wood to put underneath my door. Works like a charm.'

'Didn't you use it this time?'

'Doesn't work with sliding doors.' With a soft sigh, Mary ran her hand once more over the sweater. 'Your young man's been gone a long while.'

'He might need help.' Stacia moved toward the door. 'I'm going to find him. Just stay here. Don't go anywhere.'

'Of course, my dear, but don't you think — '

Stacia shut her ears to Mary's protest and left the room quickly. Her limbs might be stiff and her reactions dull, but it felt suddenly imperative to make sure Andrew was safe.

The door to Mary's room was open wide, but the room itself was empty. She stepped cautiously inside, and stood for a moment listening.

Where could Andrew be? Another panic, more chilling than the first, descended on her. She pressed her eyes shut and prayed it would disappear, prayed, too, that the need within would dissolve.

'Stacia?'

She opened her eyes. Quiet as a spectre, Andrew slipped through the balcony's sliding doors. He came close and touched her arm, his fingers drawing fire.

'Are you all right?' he demanded urgently. 'You look as though you've seen a ghost.'

'Just you.' She smiled shakily. 'I wondered where you had gone.'

'You were worried about me?' he asked, his own returning smile sending a current racing through her body.

'Not really,' she denied, wishing her words were true, wishing she didn't love this man she couldn't trust.

'Liar,' he said softly, touching her cheek.

'Did you find the intruder?' she asked, a blaze erupting where he touched her.

'No,' Andrew muttered. His gaze drifted around the room, pulled hers along with it.

Mary's scents and powders were lined up against the dressing table's mirror. A silver-backed brush and hand mirror lay face down before them. In the open closet, her clothes hung neatly, color coded and arranged by type; pastel-colored blouses to the left, neatly ironed skirts to the right. Nothing out of place, nothing special enough to steal.

Andrew shrugged, then glanced back to Stacia. 'Where's the sweater?' he demanded.

'In my room.'

'You left it there alone?'

'Miss Argyle's there.'

'But there's an intruder about.' He hurried through the doorway.

Stacia followed, and saw Mary at the far end of the hall, moving away from them down the corridor.

'Mary,' she cried.

The old woman turned.

'Where are you going? Are you all right?'

'I'm fine,' Mary called back, but she put her hand against the corridor wall as if to brace herself.

Stacia hurried forward, glad to have Andrew by her side.

'You seemed to be taking so long,' the old woman said as they drew near.

'We were only gone a moment.' Stacia laid her arm reassuringly around Mary's shoulders.

'I thought you might need help,' Mary continued. 'I was . . . was going to get the hotel owner.'

'I'll let him know what happened,' Andrew said. 'Come and sit for a moment.' He motioned toward Stacia's room.

Stacia walked with Mary through the narrow doorway and sat with her on the end of the bed.

'Did you find him,' the old woman

asked, staring up at Andrew with anxious eyes. Beneath Stacia's arm, her body trembled.

Andrew glanced at the sweater still clutched in Mary's hand. 'Are you positive you heard something?'

'Oh yes,' Mary said sharply. 'I'm not a senile old woman, if that's what you think.'

'We don't think anything of the sort,' Stacia reassured her.

'That's not what I meant,' Andrew said quietly. 'Tell us what happened.'

'I had a headache, so I decided to lie down. All the glare from the sun, you know.' As Mary's words spilled out, she seemed to gain confidence. 'I wore my hat and my sun glasses when I went outside, even stopped off after my stroll for a cup of tea in that restaurant along the harbor front. Had the nicest chat with the proprietor. His youngest son owns a cafe in Dorset. Rather close to where I'm from.'

'The headache?' Andrew murmured, looking dazed by the information flood.

Stacia suppressed a grin. Andrew obviously wasn't used to old women. Grandmother Roberts had prided herself on getting to the point, but even she made you feel like a mouse in a maze.

'I came back to the hotel and asked the owner's mother-in-law, a very helpful woman, I must say, if she had any headache tablets I could purchase. I felt a little dizzy and didn't feel up to braving the chemist's shop. The thought of struggling through my dictionary . . . ' Mary shuddered. 'The landlord's mother-in-law brought me a pot of tea and a very soothing balm for my forehead.'

'And the intruder?' Andrew asked.

'I drank my tea, then pulled the curtains and lay down on my bed. I must have dropped off to sleep, but a sound woke me.'

'Where was it coming from?'

'The balcony. I lay quite, quite, still.' Mary shot them a swift smile. 'I'm not sure I could have moved if I wanted to.'

Being paralyzed with fear was something Stacia could understand, or with love even, unable to move a muscle.

'What kind of sound was it?' Andrew's concentration was completely focussed on Mary and her story. His intensity seemed to fluster the older woman as much as it did Stacia. It was a power he had, a force to which women especially seemed vulnerable.

Mary flushed, and her eyebrows drew together as though she was trying to remember. 'A sort of thump,' she finally said. 'As though someone had dropped something.'

'Could it have come from the room next to yours?'

'Oh, no.' Her denial was firm. 'It was from my balcony and it was directly after the thump that I saw the shadow.'

'Shadow?' Stacia asked.

'Against my curtains. It was there for only an instant, before it disappeared.'

'Could it have been the shadow of a cloud?' Stacia suggested. That thought was preferable to the alternative of someone skulking around the hotel. At least there was no way the skulker could have been Andrew. He had been with her, opening the package.

The will, Stacia suddenly remembered, glancing at the floor. The envelope still lay where it had dropped. She picked it up and held it behind her back. A chill passed over her as she did so, as though a cloud was really there.

'It was no cloud,' Mary said indignantly. 'I may have been afraid, but I'm not blind.'

'Is there anything you have that a thief might want?' Andrew asked.

'I can't think of a thing.' The old woman shrugged. 'My money is all in traveler's cheques and I carry those with me. Mind you,' she said shrewdly, 'a burglar wouldn't know that.'

'Did he come into your room at all?' Stacia asked.

'I frightened him off,' Mary replied proudly, the pink deepening on her cheeks. 'My knitting bag was next to my bed. I picked it up, then dropped it to the floor. It made quite a noise.'

She looked so triumphant, Stacia

hadn't the heart to remind her that discretion was the safer part of valor.

'You could have been hurt,' Andrew chided.

'Perhaps so, young man, but I assumed whoever was out there would leave when they realized the room was occupied.'

'We should report this to the police,' Stacia said.

'I'll do it.' Mary stood, looking quite unlike the frightened woman who had pounded on Stacia's door just minutes before. 'And I'm going to complain to the management of this hotel. It's disgraceful when elderly women are frightened in their beds. The owner must be made to do something!' She hobbled toward the door.

Stacia swiftly followed her. 'My sweater, Mary,' she said, touching the old woman's arm.

'Gracious!' Mary said. 'I'd forgotten.' She glanced past Stacia and smiled at Andrew. 'A lovely choice, young man. Although black's not quite the color for a young woman, but it will certainly suit Stacia's skin tones. And unless I miss my guess, you paid a pretty penny for it.'

Andrew returned the smile grimly.

Stacia took the sweater from Mary and rubbed it against her cheek, hiding her face from Andrew. Her skin felt suddenly hot enough to singe the wool, and she remained motionless even after Mary passed through the door.

'So you told her I gave it to you?' he said softly.

'Of course I didn't,' she denied.

'She's under that impression.'

Stacia lowered the sweater and stared him in the eyes. 'None of that matters, Andrew.' She jutted her chin forward. 'It's time you told me the truth.'

He stepped toward her, his silhouette forbidding against the day's last light shafting in through the window.

Stacia caught her breath. No matter what he said, all joy was lost. If he took the will, he'd been lying to her all along; if he denied all knowledge, he was lying to her now.

She steadied her breathing. Whatever the outcome, she had to know.

He drew near enough to touch. Desire rose within her, as fierce as the noonday sun, and along with it came the longing to flee this room with its secrets and shadows and lie once again on the rocks. To become lost in the moment and the heat of the man. To think of nothing. To simply feel.

His hand curled around hers and she stared down at his fingers, so elegantly boned, but so much larger than her own. So much stronger, yet gentle. His fingers formed a fence, but she was confident if she moved, she could lift that barrier, that no matter who he was, they had shared something more powerful than physical strength.

They were bound in a way she could not afford, for the binding was dangerous, the illusion of safety, perilous. Grimly, she raised her gaze to his.

His eyes were steady in the waning light.

She longed to pull her hand from his and touch her fingers to the lamp switch, to illuminate his eyes and disperse the secrets of his heart. But if making love under the Mediterranean sun was unable to perform such a feat, what chance had mere electricity.

'My name is Andrew Moore,' he told her again softly. 'It isn't Andropolous. There is no will and testament.' He reached behind her back and took the envelope from her.

She cried out as he ripped it open, but inside there was simply a single piece of paper. A blank piece of paper with no writing on it.

He took the sweater from her, too, and held it up. It was beautiful in its simplicity, made of the softest wool.

'No will,' he said again. His eyes held hers like the eyes of a magician as he touched the baubles sewn to the front. They were the sweater's only decoration, simple, yet strangely fashionable.

'But there *are* diamonds,' he added. '*My* diamonds.'

10

Diamonds.

The word conjured up images of engagement rings and tiaras. Stacia snatched the sweater from Andrew's hands and moved dazedly toward the window, holding the sweater up to what remained of the light.

The baubles didn't look like diamonds. Sparkly, yes, but no more so than a piece of costume jewelry. They couldn't be diamonds. If they were, that meant . . . Her pulse hammered a staccato beat against her temple and her mouth grew as dry as the air outside. She thrust the sweater back at Andrew with shaking hands.

If these were diamonds, *she* had carried them into the country. Stacia drew the back of her hand across her wet brow. No, not carried them. Smuggled them. The room began to swim.

'Sit down,' Andrew cried, and pushed her to the bed.

Stolen goods. She had smuggled stolen goods into the country. She opened her mouth to protest that it wasn't so, then closed it again without saying a word. Black dots formed a wavy line in front of her eyes.

'Stacia. Stacia.'

A pinpoint of light appeared at the end of a long tunnel, grew larger, more distinct. A tender voice drew her to it. Something cool pressed her forehead. With relief, she leaned into it.

'It's all right,' Andrew said.

It was his arm holding her waist, keeping her from falling.

'Take a deep breath,' he instructed, 'and put your head between your knees.'

She took a breath as Andrew had suggested, but her head still spun like a merry-go-round.

Andrew's eyes, when she could focus, were dark with concern.

'I didn't steal your diamonds,' she

whispered, hoping he'd believe her. Why should he? She hadn't believed him.

'I know,' he said gently, placing a finger on her lips. 'Don't talk. Just rest.'

She wrenched her lips away. 'How do you know?' she asked.

'You got them from Wilson.'

'Stone. His name was Stone.' Her head felt as though it were going to float away from her shoulders. To steady herself, she focussed on his eyes.

'Wilson,' he countered flatly. 'My most *trusted* employee.' Andrew's mouth twisted. 'He managed my brokerage in Chicago. Was in charge of all the shipments to New York and London.'

'Brokerage?'

'Moore's Diamond Brokerage. I buy, sell, and trade.'

It was difficult to concentrate when the line of Andrew's jaw led to the sensual curve of his lips, reminding Stacia of how they'd felt kissing her mouth, making her sickeningly aware of the turn of events.

'How did you know Wilson gave the

diamonds to me?' she asked.

'I was watching his house. I was sure he'd stolen the diamonds but didn't know where he was sending them.' He took her hand in his. 'I saw you pick them up.'

'You were the man in the car,' Stacia replied slowly. At last she understood. Memory served up a quick image of the street, the car, and the battered baseball cap. She should have known him by his hat.

'I couldn't believe you had anything to do with it. You looked so young — ' He drew a circle around the inside of her palm. ' — so vulnerable. I was sure you had some other reason to be there, but when you came out of Wilson's house, you were holding a package.'

'You followed me.' She could scarcely breathe.

'I told you that at the cove.'

'It didn't make sense then.' Her body was numb. All feeling had fled and might never return. 'At the airport in Chicago, you knew who I was.'

'Not who, exactly. Not your name. Not then.'

'The airplane, Athens.' The list grew and the hurt grew with it. 'The theft of my purse.' She stared up at him, her cheeks hot. 'Was that your idea?'

'No.' A swift grin flashed on his lips. 'An unexpected bit of luck.'

'Luck!' She sprang to her feet.

'I needed to know how much you knew, how much you were involved. I needed to stay close to you.' He stood, also.

He'd suspected her, thought she was a thief. Even when they'd shared a room. Even when he'd kissed her.

'Why didn't you just take the diamonds?' Rage shook her so fiercely the pain of his duplicity dulled.

He touched her shoulder with a hand of a stranger.

'It wasn't *you* I wanted to turn over to the police,' he said bitterly. 'It was Wilson and that son-of-a-bitch at the other end.'

She noticed across a barrier of sound

and touch, the pulse steadily throbbing at the base of his throat and the exhausted shadow around his eyes. A vise squeezed her heart and she turned away.

'But it was *me* you followed,' she protested, close to tears. '*Me* you befriended.'

'You could lead me to the rest of the thieves.'

'It was *me* you made love to.' She choked on the words. 'You used me. Manipulated me.' Her voice dropped to a whisper. 'You lied to me.'

'I told you my name. I couldn't tell you anything else.'

'You didn't trust me.'

'Did you trust me?'

She swallowed hard, remembered her fear and suspicions.

'Besides — ' He released her suddenly. 'I had to keep you safe.'

'Safe!' she repeated disgustedly.

'If you were innocent, you were in danger.' He kneaded his forehead with his knuckles. 'But it doesn't matter anymore.'

'What do you mean?'

'It's over.'

'Nothing's over. I haven't delivered the package yet.'

'And you're not going to.'

'Yes, I am.'

'I won't let you.'

'You can't stop me.'

His gaze held hers, his expression unfathomable.

'I have to,' she insisted.

'Why?' He said it patiently.

'Because I'm not a criminal.' She tried to breathe naturally, to stop this dreadful sucking in of air. 'Because you're after the person I'm supposed to deliver this to. I have to help. I owe you.'

'This isn't your fault. I don't want you at risk.'

She turned away, but his gaze warmed her back, insinuating her space and weakening her resolve. She stepped toward the window, away from him and his power.

'I told you before,' she said, her

throat tight. 'My safety is not your concern.'

She heard his sharp intake of breath and heard him move. At any moment she expected his hand to touch her shoulder. Instead, a knock sounded.

Andrew got to the door first, and flung it open so hard it crashed against the wall. It was no porter this time holding a message, not even a shy-faced maid. The much wrinkled face of the hotel owner's mother-in-law stared in through the doorway, her raven eyes bright against her brown skin. The only color on the unrelieved black of her person was the pink of her cheeks. With claw-like fingers, she held out a note to Stacia.

* * *

The taverna wasn't fancy, but Andrew wasn't in the mood for fancy. He wanted a place they could pretend to be tourists, one small enough for him to watch Stacia's back.

'Act naturally,' he said gruffly. 'If they're watching, and they probably are, we don't want them to know we're on to them.'

The black smudges that were Stacia's eyes widened, but she nodded in agreement.

'We'll go in, have dinner — ' He smiled at her reassuringly and wished for the millionth time that they were just as they pretended, a man and a woman going out for the evening. ' — perhaps dance a little.'

'Is this necessary?' she asked.

'Yes,' he said firmly. He had tried in the hotel room to make her understand, had told her that for some, diamonds were worth the killing. He thought of Nancy and his palms grew clammy. What had happened to his wife could not happen again.

He placed his hand on Stacia's back and steered her toward a corner table, her body rigid beneath his fingers. Backs to the wall. Safer that way. She might not be happy with what he'd decided, but that was too damned bad.

'I'm glad you've decided to be sensible,' he said. It was him, not her, who would meet Andropolous tomorrow.

'You didn't leave me any choice.' She frowned at him through the glow of the candle on the table between them.

'No,' he said repressively. He didn't want to go through the arguments again, was not willing to spend their few remaining hours together fighting.

'Tell me again why I can't go,' she demanded.

'Andropolous won't be expecting me. Might not know who I am.' Even as Andrew said it, the possibility seemed remote. 'I'll rent a skiff, go over early, stake the place out.' Perhaps going over the details one more time was good. It would let her feel involved without exposing her to danger. Earlier her eyes had taken on a stubborn look that frightened him.

'He said I was to meet him at the fortress on Spinalonga Island.' She pronounced the Greek name haltingly. 'Seems an isolated place to meet. Do you think he suspects we're on to him?' Her clear eyes demanded an honest answer.

He shrugged, no longer able to lie.

Her gaze narrowed. 'You *are* taking the police?'

'And tell them what? That I'm after jewel thieves. I'm the one who has the diamonds.' Diamonds Stacia had brought into the country illegally. 'I have to go myself.'

He had to go for Nancy, for Stacia too. 'Besides, the police are useless.' He stood. 'Forget it for now. We're supposed to be having a good time.'

He held out his hand. 'Dance?'

For an instant she hesitated, then put her hand in his. He pulled her into his arms and it felt as though he'd come home. She intoxicated him, entranced him, filled him with desire. Made him crave for this manhunt he'd embarked upon to be over.

Her breasts brushed his chest and he

felt her nipples harden. With a cry, she drew back.

Stacia pushed against his arms. She could no longer dance with Andrew and hide how hurt she felt. So far the evening had passed in a tension-filled blur of food and wine, but she couldn't feel his body next to hers knowing she was just a pawn in his diamond game.

He had used her, manipulated her, and in the end on that rock, against her better judgement, against all that she knew or guessed, she had handed him her heart. She'd been wrong to do that. Safety didn't come in numbers, particularly didn't come in twos. If you wanted to be free from pain, you were best off alone.

Stacia fought back the tears that welled in her eyes, but they refused to go away, half blinding her with their moisture. Andrew suddenly released her hand. She stood motionless, bewildered, so engrossed in hiding her emotions, she'd been unaware the music had changed. Until now, rock tunes from another continent and an earlier decade had reverberated through the room. Now, in its place, came the insistent sound of Crete.

With a start, Stacia noticed that most of the tourists had left. With their leaving, an ancient energy had emerged. A power, a love of life, one so all encompassing it was embodied in the pulse of the music, the sensual gyration of hips, the ruby red of the wine, and the joyfully intense smiles of the Greek dancers around them.

Andrew held up his hands, palms toward her. Hypnotized, she raised her hands also. Their palms touched, yet didn't touch, were apart, yet together, more a connection of auras and a fusing of spirits than two people joined in dance.

She'd never danced like this before, as though her legs were controlled like some puppet on a string. Her feet had never been this sure of movement in the past, had never known so completely where to go. The music drove her before it, lifting her feet and her heart.

It stirred her breast and loins, brought heat to her cheeks.

A current flowed in the space between her and Andrew, and brought with it a thread of joy demanding acknowledgement. She smiled at him, not wanting to, but unable to resist, and he returned her smile so warmly the pain in her heart receded to a dull ache in her chest.

Then the music quickened and the couples merged into two lines; one of women and one of men. Still, they didn't falter.

Andrew wove in and out on the periphery of her vision, his face, chest and legs blurred by the shadowy light and the fluid movements of the dancers. But his eyes met hers in a constant, steady gaze. He welded her to him in the weightless jubilation of the dance.

When the music finally ended, he was opposite her again, tall, solid and devastatingly desirable. He held out his hand and for a long moment she simply stared at it. But in the end she clenched her fist and walked away.

He caught up with her before she reached the door, his fingers touching her shoulder with the strength of steel.

Stacia shuddered, overwhelmed with longing and utter despair.

11

Stacia noiselessly opened the door of her room and peered through the crack. No one in the hall beyond. She should be happy about that, but fear snaked down her spine.

She edged through the door, the soles of her running shoes squeaking on the hall's tiled floor. She held the plastic bag containing the package carefully, not wanting the paper inside to crackle. She had to convince Andrew to take her with him, something he would never do if she had the package on her. She would pretend all she carried was bread and cheese, something to eat after their meeting with Andropolous was over.

The package was the only weapon they had. If Andrew got into trouble, if he couldn't subdue Andropolous as he believed he could, she would offer the villain the diamonds and buy their safe passage back to Agios Nikolaos. Andrew would get what he wanted, would know who Andropolous really was ... but he'd be safe, and that was all that mattered to her.

She paused in front of Andrew's door, suddenly afraid to knock. He wouldn't want to take her, but that was too damned bad. Andropolous played to win. Meeting him alone was crazy. If Andrew persisted in refusing to call the police, she'd leave him no choice but to use her as a back-up. All she had to do was convince him of that.

Stacia glanced at her watch. Seven o'clock. Andropolous's note had said to meet him at nine. Andrew had told her last night he intended to leave at eight, saying that would leave plenty of time to find a fisherman willing to boat him across the water separating Crete from Spinalonga Island, then wait like a Venetian taxi until he was done.

According to the guide book, the fortress itself was Venetian, an imposing stone structure that guarded the Mirabello Gulf. It also said that early in this century it had been used to house lepers. It seemed appropriate, somehow, that it was here they'd meet Andropolous, a lonely spot already resonant with misery and fear.

At least, she wouldn't be alone. Andrew would be there. Andropolous, too. Goose bumps rose on Stacia's arms.

Hastily, she tapped on Andrew's door. No answer. She tapped harder. Still no response. She laid her ear against the wood, but heard no sound within, no shower water running or rustling of clothes. Her heart skipped a beat. He must have left already, must have gone without her.

She turned and sped toward the stairs, taking them two at a time, her fingers trailing the railing, ready to clutch at it if she stumbled. She prayed that with movement her mind might stop its racing, stop visualizing the ways Andropolous might hurt her, and forget how Andrew already had.

She only slowed when she reached the lobby. She nodded sedately to Mr. Stefanos at the reception desk, but was careful not to look in his direction. This cutting off of other people was not what she'd intended for this trip, but it was necessary now if she wanted to avoid questions.

A brisk breeze blew in from the sea and up the narrow street to the hotel. When Stacia stepped outdoors, her shirt flattened against her chest. She wrapped her arms around her body, trying to give herself warmth. If she went back for a sweater now, she might not find the courage to embark again.

The nearer she got to the marina, the more she wished she was anywhere else on earth. The ache in her chest had spread and left her numb. Better that way. Easier to bear than being able to feel.

Not as many skiffs bobbed alongside the dock as she'd imagined there would be. Where was Andrew? Her fingers closed convulsively on the handle of her bag. Had he already gone? She should have realized from the fresh fish in the restaurants they had passed yesterday morning that the fishermen would be up and out on the water before dawn.

Taking Andrew with them.

Had he lied to her? Been so determined she not come, that he'd given her the wrong time?

At the far end of the cement dock, one boat remained. It was bright blue, the color of the sea and the color of Andrew's eyes. Stiffening her resolve, she moved toward it. She would follow Andrew to the island and meet him there. Might be better that way. No convincing to be done.

The fisherman in the boat was short but broad-chested. The red scarf he wore jauntily around his neck relieved the unrelenting black of his attire.

Stacia approached him. She prayed he would think her merely eccentric, a crazy tourist with an unusual request for this time of the morning, *not* see her as a smuggler with a package full of diamonds.

Smiles, gestures, *parakalo, ne, ochi.* The extent of Stacia's linguistic fluency was reached within seconds. But in the end she settled in the bow of the fishing boat and moved with it as it chugged its way across the water. A long, narrow island loomed before her in the early morning translucence like a home for the *Cyclopes.*

The fortress grew larger as they drew near, towered over the bare land surrounding it in a threatening mound of grey stone. Windowless slits, like empty eye sockets, dotted the walls and stared down at her, seemed to be daring her to approach.

There was no sign of Andrew. His boat must be moored at a different cove than the one they aimed for. This cove was perfect with its clear water and sandy beach, unusual on this coastline of rocks and crevices. Only the fortress rising on the cliff beyond spoiled the view. The fortress, and the terror it promised.

She could only imagine the man she had come to meet; swarthy and paunchy, strong and intimidating, or perhaps clean shaven and educated, someone with the brains and guts to pull off such a theft.

The skiff crunched against the cove's gravel bottom. Stacia glanced at her watch and frowned. Eight o'clock. It had taken longer than she had expected to get here. Andropolous could be here already, though there was no sign of him, either, no movement, no boat. With a tight-lipped smile, she thanked the fisherman and scanned the sea beyond his shoulder. Still no sign of Andrew. He must be up at the fortress.

She gestured to the fisherman to wait and started up the narrow path. The higher she got, the more lightheaded she became. Only a mountain goat would enjoy this view. She didn't like heights. She'd found that out one summer when she begged her boyfriend of the moment to take her climbing. She had frozen in the middle of the cliff, unable to go up, or down, or sideways. Her boyfriend had encouraged and cajoled, but nothing he said convinced her it was safe to move. She clung to the rock face, her fingers frozen in place until a park ranger edged across to rescue her.

Stacia shuddered, glad this cliff had a trail. If she was able to fight the urge to look down, she might not be undone as she'd been before. Though looking up was just as bad. The vision of clear, blue sky atop an unending line of grey granite was dizzying in the extreme.

The urge to check her bearings came again, and she succumbed to a swift glance below.

Her boat was leaving!

She moved too suddenly. An avalanche of gravel flew from beneath her feet and skittered down the trail. She shouted, her voice pitched abnormally high with shock. The sound echoed off the rocks and bounced back at her. The taxiing fisherman, already clear of the shallow water, glanced up at her and waved.

'Come back,' Stacia screamed again, gesturing wildly with her arm.

The fisherman waved back, grinning cheerfully up at her. He obviously didn't understand her any better than she had him. With his engine going, he probably couldn't even hear her voice, and she could do nothing but watch helplessly as the boat put-putted its way back to Agios Nikolaos.

The package she carried seemed suddenly too heavy, the urge to retreat overwhelming. But if she bolted when the going got tough, Andrew would have to face the danger alone. Dismally, she faced the rocky trail and took another step upward.

The path narrowed further, but by squinting her eyes to block out the view she made it to the top. A short walk along a grassy knoll and suddenly she was there.

The fortress appeared eerily, frighteningly, empty, with nary a guard or ticket taker, or even an old crone intent on cleaning ancient corridors.

Stacia had a sudden sickening intuition she was already too late, that she'd find

Andrew lying within, perhaps beaten and tied up. She stepped through the open archway and into the dim shadow of the building, certain that at any moment an alarm might ring or sirens blare, warning Andropolous she had arrived.

The crude map Andropolous had sent her was a mess of dashes and squiggles. She studied it closely, even turned it upside down in an attempt to make sense of it, but that gesture simply increased its maze-like confusion.

The old guard room had to be down the narrow passage on her left. Stacia glanced back at the map and hoped she was wrong. There was no place there to hide, no nook to enter should she need it, no cranny to crouch within if she felt danger. With the worn smoothness of the passage's walls, she'd be as exposed as a clay duck in a shooting gallery.

She shook her head, but couldn't dispel the haunting images of death and destruction. The thoughts clung to her like the cobwebs on the surrounding walls, the result of too many movies and too many books.

Stacia squared her shoulders. She was a fool to imagine the worst. She would walk down the passage, find Andrew, and wait with him until Andropolous arrived. Arriving first would put them in a position of power, and make it possible to initiate a sensible discussion with sensible solutions.

And if Andrew wasn't there yet, she'd pretend to know nothing, would simply hand over the package and get out. But she would know who Andropolous was and be able to describe him to Andrew.

Most importantly, she'd be able to prevent Andrew from being the one to confront Andropolous. If he wasn't there to lose his temper, he would not get shot at, injured, or worse. He would be *safe*.

Stacia smiled faintly as the dreaded word insinuated itself into her brain. It wasn't nearly so dreadful when applied to someone she cared about.

Panic appeared from nowhere, scattering her resolve. She had realized at the villa that she cared for Andrew, but not to this extent. She touched her fingers to her throat, felt the cording of her neck muscles and the vibration of soundless protest. Splaying her fingers up and over her lips, she was stunned to find that no sound emerged. Only a whisper of air entered then departed again swiftly.

She pressed her lips resolutely tight and dropped her hands to her sides, waiting and praying for the hammering of her heart to slow, and the incessant pounding of blood in her head to silence. Finally, she breathed in two deep breaths, and forced her feet forward, not walking steadfastly down the middle as she had envisioned, but rather ghost-like along the wall, one hand outstretched to touch the cool, soothing stone beneath her fingertips.

Mid-way down the passage she paused and held the map up to the light shafting in through the dimness from one high window. The first room on her right had to be the one she searched for.

Two feet, four, ten, and she was there.

She expelled her breath slowly, her lungs close to bursting from holding in the air. Though she still saw no one, she was afraid to make a sound.

With her cheeks sucked in between her teeth, she edged open the heavy door to the room. Stale air met her nostrils, and the damp musky scent you might find in a cave.

'Good morning, Miss Roberts.'

Stacia pushed the door wider, her heart skipping mid beat at the sound of her name.

'Miss Argyle!' she exclaimed. Adrenaline, too long held, fled Stacia's body. Her strength drained with it. Her knees came close to crumpling and her arms fell limply to her sides. She stared with relief at the elderly woman opposite, standing against the far wall, capacious handbag on the floor beside her.

'I didn't think anyone was here,' Stacia said. *Except Andrew. Where was he?* She attempted to cross the space between them, but her body refused to cooperate.

'You're right. It's early,' Miss Argyle said, her voice holding a trace of amusement.

'You have to leave,' Stacia urged, her previous panic surging back. 'I'm meeting someone here.' Heat flooded her face. 'I — ' She couldn't explain it to Miss Argyle, no matter how afraid she was that the older woman would end up in the middle.

'That young man I've seen you with?' the older woman prompted.

'No . . . yes . . . ' Stacia stammered.

'Is he coming?' A faint smile lingered on Miss Argyle's lips, but her pleasant expression didn't extend to her eyes.

Uncertainty gripped Stacia.

'Is he?' Miss Argyle demanded again, more insistently this time.

A sudden, incomprehensible inclination to lie overwhelmed Stacia, to do anything to keep the truth hidden from this woman. But how could she lie when she didn't know what to say.

'No. . .o,' she said slowly, her stomach churning, but her gaze never wavering from Miss Argyle's face. For an instant, something new flickered in the older woman's eyes. Relief? Satisfaction? It didn't matter. Somehow, intuitively, Stacia knew she'd said the right thing.

'Good.' The unsteady wobble of age disappeared with the word, leaving Mary Argyle's voice firmer, more youthful in tone.

A clammy chill jacketed Stacia's body.

'You have something for me, I believe.' Mary Argyle stepped closer. Her walk was different also, her step more limber.

Miss Argyle's determination caused the dread to roar up Stacia's spine and a claustrophobic fear seeped into her pores. Like some dreadful disease, the fear traveled through her veins, first heating, then freezing, then immobilizing her body.

She shrank against the door jamb, wanting only to run, yet certain that if she did, something dreadful would occur. Something more terrible than standing and waiting for a woman she no longer knew, to reach her.

She longed for the comfort of Andrew's arms and the strength of his hand holding on to hers. But his touch seemed as distant from this woman and this place as the sun in the sky seemed remote from the earth.

'What do you want?' Stacia whispered, her lips so dry the words came out cracked.

'You *know* what I want.' Miss Argyle halted beside a desk, the room's only piece of furniture, a modern incongruity in the presence of the past. 'Now,' she commanded, holding out her hand for Stacia's bag.

'I was meant to deliver this to Mr. Andropolous,' Stacia said. She slid her arms behind her back, putting her tote bag and the package out of sight.

If she pretended the original instructions still stood, perhaps even now there was some escape. Some return to innocence. Some possibility she could simply hand over the package and be let go.

Perhaps even now her fear could be hidden, the sheen of sweat erupting on her body somehow made invisible.

Miss Argyle's answering laugh was loud in the echoing emptiness of the room. Whether it penetrated the thick stone of the fortress, Stacia was uncertain, but one thing she did know. She had never felt so alone.

'There is no Mr. Andropolous,' Mary Argyle said.

She had known since the day before that Andropolous was a fake, but she didn't want Miss Argyle to take his place. A humming began in Stacia's ears, blocking the starkness of the older woman's words, but nothing could disguise the contempt on Miss Argyle's face.

Stacia squared her shoulders and willed her body to move, only to find that when she tried she couldn't force her feet to action.

She pressed her lips together and with a great effort of will, repositioned her tote bag and squeezed it, feeling the package inside. It reassured her to know she still had it in her hands, that she hadn't simply handed it over at Mary Argyle's command.

'Miss Argyle,' she began, steadying her gaze on the older woman's face. She needed to know the truth, even if it was the last thing she'd ever know.

'Stupid name!' the older woman spat out.

Stacia stared at her, dazed.

'That's not my real name,' Mary Argyle continued.

'What is?'

Mary's lips widened into a parody of a smile. 'Not that. Not some stupid English name.' Satisfaction gleamed from her eyes. 'There's no harm in telling you now — '

An icy finger of fear threaded its way across Stacia's shoulders and slid down her back . . .

' — as you'll not be telling anyone else.'

. . . then lodged at the base of her spine, locking her to the cold stone floor.

'Maria Argolis,' the older woman introduced herself proudly, sweeping a lock of grey hair back from her face.

'Why go by a false name?' Stacia spoke the words forcefully to rid her voice of any quaver, wishing she had the power to dent the other woman's satisfaction.

Maria's face took on the look of a ferret, too sharp and cunning to be human. 'Your precious Mr. Moore would have recognized the name Argolis.' Maria's clipped British accent disappeared as swiftly as a chameleon changes color, the more melodic Greek tones taking its place.

'He's had dealings with my brother,' Maria continued. 'Ruined him. Sent him to jail.' Her mouth hardened. 'My brother was stupid, of course, getting caught with the diamonds.' She gave a snort of disgust. 'He deserves to rot in jail if he can't follow instructions.' Her face took on a gloating expression. 'They couldn't pin the murder on him though. He hadn't done that. I didn't dare let him. He'd have messed it up one way or another.'

'What murder?' Stacia whispered.

'Never mind,' Maria snapped. Her blue eyes were no longer vague with age, but had darkened to the color of glistening black slate.

'If he didn't do it, who did?' Stacia asked.

'I did,' Maria said. 'Now give me the package.'

Stacia's arms went rigid. Her bag suddenly felt sharp-edged and stiff against her fingers. Her legs seemed to have no feeling in them at all, no blood, sinew, or nerves, nothing to allow her to twist through the door and race down the passage toward freedom.

Her mind flashed transitorily to Andrew, the memory of his steady eyes and comforting touch helping her to draw in a calming breath. She readied herself, felt her muscles coil and tighten, willed her face to become impassive. She could allow no muscle, no twitching nerve or flickering eye to indicate her intention to flee. She had what she had come for, the identity of Andropolous, and now she had to get that information to Andrew.

Resting one hand against the door jamb, she held her gaze low, ready to duck and twirl, whirl and run.

'I wouldn't try it if I were you,' Maria's terrifying voice continued.

Stacia's right eye twitched and panic welled in her belly. Slowly, carefully, she lifted her head, and the hammering of her heart ceased as she stared down the cold, metallic barrel of a pistol.

She knew her eyes had widened from the sudden chill in their corners and the wetness of collecting moisture.

'The package,' Maria Argolis demanded, holding the gun steady and pointing it at her.

'Why didn't you take it when you had the chance?' Stacia asked. 'At the hotel? You could have taken it then.'

'I tried,' Maria said coldly, 'but you came back too soon.' She raised the gun higher. 'I imagine you're sorry about that now.'

Stacia fought to capture a breath, to force at least some air into her lungs. If she concentrated on one limb at a time, perhaps she could will her body to move. She slowly lifted her arm and brought her tote bag into view. She didn't want to look at it, didn't have to actually see it to know she had failed.

Unable to take her gaze off the gun, she stared down its sleek length and imagined the thud the bullet would make in her chest. It was as if it had already happened, the pain there was so excruciating.

She'd thought nothing could be worse than knowing Andrew had used her, that he'd made love to her and helped her, with just one goal in mind, retrieving his diamonds. But she'd been wrong.

Within minutes, perhaps seconds, a bullet would blast from that pistol and she'd never see Andrew again. *That* would be the worst thing.

In slow motion, as if it were someone else's arm altogether, Stacia observed her arm lift and extend the tote bag outward. With an ominous click, Maria Argolis cocked the gun, took the proffered bag, and backed away.

So Maria's neat grey pant suit wouldn't be spattered with blood, Stacia thought dully. She stood far enough away to remain clean and tidy. Nothing to connect the woman opposite with the violence the pistol promised.

'It's too bad it has to end this way,' Maria said coldly, her voice detached, and clinical, as though Stacia was about to be fired from a job, not murdered in cold blood. Maria pulled the package out of the bag, ripped it open, and shook out the sweater. The diamonds sparkled against the black wool, catching what little light came into the area.

Rage flared heat across Stacia's cheeks and down the icy length of her neck and chest, cutting through the misty, swirling oblivion. She couldn't just let this happen, couldn't allow this woman to shoot without somehow trying to stop her. Stacia raised her hand and held her palm outward, as though her flesh alone could stop the attack.

'I regret it's necessary to shoot you,' Maria said tauntingly, 'but you do understand, don't you, that I can't allow you to tell anyone about me.'

'I won't tell anyone,' Stacia promised. She held her body rigid, determined to stop herself from sinking to the floor on knees too weak to hold her.

'You won't have the opportunity,' the other woman replied sharply.

'They'll find you,' Stacia cried. 'I expect the police will arrive any minute now.' If only that were true.

Argolis's finger tightened on the trigger.

The hair rose on the back of Stacia's neck.

'Crete is a small place,' she whispered, her gaze glued to the gun. If she watched it, perhaps it wouldn't go off. 'There's nowhere to hide.' If she kept talking, perhaps some miracle would occur.

The older woman smiled, the cold,

cruel smile of a crocodile about to pronounce its meal delicious. 'I have a boat,' she said, 'and a man to run it.' She gave a rueful shrug. 'He's not overly bright, but he can get me off this island.' Her eyes were coldly triumphant. 'I have a safe place to hide on Crete.'

Stacia's breath grew so shallow, her chest barely rose. Then something familiar touched her from behind. Andrew's hand, whose warm cautionary pressure on her waist warned her to be silent.

Maria Argolis backed toward a small door on the opposite wall. '*Adio*,' she said softly. With a slight movement of her finger, she pressed the trigger.

A flash, a puff of smoke, and a flicker of white streaked across Stacia's vision, while at the same time, a sharp pain lanced her side. If there was more to it than that, Stacia didn't know what. All she could see now was an edging of moss growing in a crack between the stones on which she lay. Her shoulder ached as if wrenched from its socket and the blast echoed again and again in the space reserved for her brain.

Someone groaned, a door slammed shut, and a silence ensued, so complete, so unexpected, she was sure she was dead.

12

Another groan, coinciding so completely with Stacia's pain, that she knew without doubt it was coming from her.

She was alive.

With intense concentration she managed to separate the solid green of the moss into individual filigreed bits. When she squinted, her vision cleared further. The whole uneven sweep of floor and one wall stretched out before her.

Her one arm lay in front of her face like the limb of a discarded doll, while the other lay pinned beneath her body, where it had turned completely numb. She tentatively wiggled the fingers of the hand she could see.

Another groan, then came the sound of something scraping the floor behind her.

'Stacia,' a voice said urgently. A warm hand touched her hip.

Blood raced to her head and cleared it.

'Andrew.' Relief he was alive resonated through her bones.

'Thank God,' Andrew said, his words muffled as though spoken through clenched teeth.

The length of his body came up against hers. She hadn't realized she was so cold until his warmth seared her back. She longed to shut her eyes and revel in that warmth, shut out this nightmare and return to their paradise on the rocks.

Andrew shifted and rose to a sitting position, forcing Stacia to sit up, too. She turned to face him and found her head spun from the movement. Shutting her eyes to maintain her bearings, she struggled to keep from folding beneath a new wave of dizziness. The pain in her shoulder helped. She focussed on it, determined to keep her lips from crying Andrew's name.

He touched her cheek, his fingers lingering and caressing.

'Are you all right,' he demanded softly.

'Yes,' Stacia whispered, opening her eyes.

Andrew's face was pale despite his tan, with pain etched in the circles around his eyes and in the lines at the corners of his compressed lips. He touched her shoulder. She bit her lip. Was unable to contain a moan.

'You're hurt. When I pushed you aside — ' Andrew's eyes grew tortured. ' — there was no time to be gentle.'

'Pushed me aside?' Memory flooded back, of him shouting first then pushing her hard to the floor. 'You saved my life,' she said breathlessly.

'Risked it,' he growled. Muscles along his jaw line tightened, and his eyes suddenly blazed. 'What the hell are you doing out here anyway?'

'Getting the answers you need. I thought you were here already.' Stacia pushed her hair back from her face. 'I thought it would be safer if we did this together.'

'If anything happened to you — ' Andrew stared at her fiercely, looking as though he longed to shake her.

'It would have had nothing to do with you.'

'It would have had everything to do with me.' He stood. 'I want you to stay here this time.'

'Where are you going?'

'To catch a thief.' Andrew's eyes turned cold as ice.

'A few diamonds are not worth getting killed over.'

'Those few diamonds are worth half a million dollars,' he growled.

Stacia gasped. 'Why didn't you tell me before?'

'You felt bad enough already. Besides, you might have insisted on helping me.' He glowered at her. 'Looks like you did that anyway.'

'But she has a gun,' Stacia protested, memories flooding back of the gun pointed at her.

'She's not a very good shot,' Andrew said, with a grim smile. 'Besides, without the diamonds, my business is destroyed.'

'She's already gone.'

'She can't have gone far.'

Stacia grabbed him by his shirt, then dropped her hold as her fingers met something slippery and warm.

Andrew groaned.

'You've been shot!' Stacia cried, staring at the blood on her hand. 'With the bullet that was meant for me.' Carefully, she pulled away his shirt. Impossible, with all the blood, to tell if the bullet had lodged in his shoulder.

Andrew shrugged away her hand and took her face between his palms. 'Stay here,' he repeated, locking her gaze with his.

Mutely, she shook her head.

His touch told her he was angry as did the taut line of his face.

'My wife died,' he growled. 'I don't want that to happen to you.'

Stacia tugged her face free. Tears gathered and threatened to spill.

'If anything more happens to you, Andrew, I — '

'Don't worry,' he said gently. 'Nothing's going to happen to me.'

'You don't know that. Nobody knows that.'

He squeezed her shoulder. 'I'll be back,' he swore, then moved toward the door through which Maria had escaped. When he reached it, he turned and looked at Stacia, blood seeping through his shirt from his wound. He stared at her hard as though memorizing her face, then disappeared like a ghost in the morning mist.

She remained motionless and listened as he ran along the stone floor. When the last sound died, she moved swiftly after him.

No matter what he said, she had to follow. No matter how much she was afraid, she had to be strong.

The door through which he'd exited led into another room identical to the first, then through to a passageway leading to an inside courtyard. Across a postage stamp square of tramped-down dirt was an archway to the outside.

At the archway, Stacia hesitated, willed the racing of her heart to slow. If she was to help Andrew, she had to be calm, had to stop her mind serving up images of him shot and bleeding, with Maria Argolis and her not-so-clever-but-strong-and-capable man standing over him. With a shudder, Stacia peered out through the archway.

Nothing.

Not a sign or sound.

Her breathing deteriorated to irregular gasps. She pulled in a long breath and tried to think. She had seen no sign of Maria's boat when she landed, so there must be another cove. A trail traced the cliff's edge, but Stacia couldn't see how far it went. Her view was blocked by the outjutting tower of the fortress.

She started along the trail, sprinting as swiftly as she dared over the uneven ground. Within seconds, she had rounded the tower. In that instant, her blood froze.

Andrew was in front of her, his muscular form listing to the right as he favored his wound. A lump lodged in

Stacia's throat, cutting off her respiration as her eyes blurred with tears. She could scarcely see him now. Scrubbing away the tears with the back of her hand, his image cleared, then blurred, then cleared again.

Too clear. Beyond Andrew was Maria, who raced like a young woman along the edge of the cliff. Her footsteps were no longer shaky or infirm. Under that false grey hair she must be far younger than she pretended. Thirty-eight or forty, perhaps. Forty-five at the most.

Past Maria, the figure of a man rose up from beyond the cliff. Stacia's heart stopped. The man must be on another trail to the sea. Must be coming to Maria's aid. Stacia's mouth opened in a panic-filled scream.

At the sound of her cry, Andrew turned toward her, his black hair whipped against his face by the wind.

A shot rang out, smoke curling from the gun in Maria's helper's hand. Stacia screamed again and began to run, ignoring the ache in her wrenched shoulder.

Andrew. Andrew. His name beat a tattoo in Stacia's skull. At least he hadn't been hit by the man's bullet. Instead, he put himself between the gunman and her, running back towards her, frantically waving her away.

Maria's helper didn't retreat, but came closer, instead, and with a sickening lurch in her belly, Stacia recognized him.

The man from the taverna. She should have guessed he was the man in Maria Argolis's pay. If Andrew hadn't come along, his diamonds would have been in Maria's hands much sooner, and if that had been the case, perhaps no one would have been hurt.

The man crouched low and aimed once more, using one hand to hold the other steady, his face hard with concentration. Maria Argolis still ran towards her helper, glancing over her shoulder as she drew near him. Her face glowed with triumph.

As Stacia ran, too, her breath rasped in her ear, drowning out the wild pounding of her heart. She didn't know what she would do to help when she finally reached Andrew, only knew that whatever happened, she had to be at his side.

'Go back!' Andrew shouted.

Stacia ignored him, continued to run, didn't dare look to her right where the cliff face was sheer for fear she would falter.

With no conscious thought, she ran on furiously, saw the man aim his gun at her, and Andrew fling himself between. She clung to the faith that if they just were together, everything would be all right.

They would both be safe.

She was closer to Andrew now, and realized with horror that the sticky patch of blood on his shoulder had spread to his rib cage. He held out his hand as though to shield her, and she drew strength from the memory of his fingers enclosing hers.

Then another shot rang out and the whole world changed.

She saw the dust first, a skittering twister of fine sand rising from the ground next to her feet. Then another shot, and another, and the ground fell away. The disappearing earth yawned emptily beside her.

She scrabbled on the cliff's edge, her feet dancing in the wind. But there was nothing left to hold her.

Andrew flew over the ground, reaching for her again, extending his fingers in a final impossible attempt to catch her. His guttural cry was the last sound she heard before she scraped and slid and bumped over the rocks.

Falling. For what seemed an eternity, she continued to fall. When finally she stopped, she lay on her back, stunned, afraid to move, speak, or even open her eyes. Only the sound of Andrew's voice penetrated her terror.

'Stacia,' he called again.

She forced her eyes open. Andrew stared down at her from the new edge of the cliff some eight feet above.

'I'm all right,' she whispered.

'Anything broken?' he asked urgently, his skin devoid of color, his gaze never leaving hers. His lips were a grim slash, as though he, too, were holding his breath, convinced, the same as she, that the whole ledge would come tumbling down if he let her out of his sight.

It was impossible to contemplate checking for broken bones. She'd have to move to do that, and movement was impossible. She remained where she was, frozen against the ledge.

'Wiggle your toes,' Andrew instructed, 'or your fingers. Anything.'

She had to do it. If only for him. Slowly, so slowly she was not positive her body obeyed her brain, Stacia wiggled the fingers of first her right hand, then her left. Her toes were next. She couldn't see them, but she could feel them curl inside her runners.

Nothing really hurt. Not if she discounted the gash on her temple dripping blood into her hair, and the cuts and scrapes she knew existed from the burning sensation they created.

Crack!

Another bullet ricocheted off the cliff above her, and a handful of gravel rumbled down, sprinkling Stacia with a fine layer of pebbles and sand. She flattened further against the hard rock and Andrew's head drew out of sight. For a long moment, there was no sound at all.

'Andrew!' She screamed.

Andrew's face reappeared, his eyes black bullets of fury as he stared along the cliff. Stacia raised her head infinitesimally and followed Andrew's gaze. Maria and her helper were half way down the other cliff trail, scrambling with more speed than care.

Every few feet, Maria halted and took aim. Another shot sung out, but the angle was poor. It hit an outjutting piece of limestone far beyond Stacia. Another shot followed in swift succession, and a loud voice shouted something incomprehensible.

Stacia cautiously raised her head higher, saw Maria's man crack open his gun and swear again. He turned to Maria, but she shook her head and showed him her own gun. Another stream of pebbles rattled down from above.

'Are you all right?' Andrew called.

With a hard swallow, she nodded. 'I think they're out of bullets, Andrew.'

'I see that,' he said.

'Go after them,' she cried, though she didn't want him to leave. 'You have to get your diamonds back.'

'I'm not going anywhere.'

'They're worth too much to lose. You said so yourself.'

'I'm not leaving you.'

'They're not armed anymore.'

He didn't move.

When Stacia stared upward, all she could see of Andrew were his broad shoulders, muscular arms, and of course his face.

'You're afraid,' she whispered, unable to believe it, but staring into his eyes, she saw the truth of her accusation.

'Not of losing my diamonds,' he replied grimly. His eyes darkened to a mask that kept his emotions secret.

'Andrew,' she moaned, heard the desperation in her own voice. She clenched a handful of sand from the ground beside her, and tried again to speak, more softly this time. 'They'll get away,' she entreated.

'It doesn't matter,' he said.

'It has to matter.' She started crying and couldn't seem to stop.

Maria and her helper were almost to the bottom of the cliff now, the movement of their feet sending avalanches of dirt sliding down before them. Maria still clutched the package and the man his useless gun. Every few yards, they looked back, as though amazed no one was following, that Andrew wasn't after what was now possible to get.

'I'm not going anywhere until you are off that ledge and safe,' Andrew called down, his voice drawing Stacia back from her contemplation of their enemy.

Safe. The one thing she'd sworn to renounce. The one thing she now wished for them both with all of her heart.

'Can you sit up?' Andrew asked. His stomach churned when he looked down and knew he couldn't go to her, that his weight would break away the ledge upon which she rested.

She smiled at him faintly. 'If you promise they won't throw stones next.'

'I'll throw them back if they do.' He tried not to hear the engine of Maria's boat sputter to life in the distance.

'Your last chance,' Stacia said, her eyes begging him to desert her. 'They're leaving!'

'Let's get you up from there,' he replied. 'I need to hold you.'

Pink tinged her cheeks.

'But you have to sit up,' he added.

Her lips opened as though she were about to say she couldn't, then she pressed them tightly shut and slowly eased herself into a sitting position.

Only once did she glance below before swiftly averting her gaze.

Andrew glanced at the sea also. What had once been inviting now presented danger. The sea's edge was far below and covered with rocks, and that's where Stacia would land if she fell from her ledge.

'Can you stand?' he asked, pushing away all images of her not making it back into his arms.

She shook her head.

'You have to do it.' He'd do it for her if only he could.

Stacia's skin paled as though she were suddenly engulfed by dizziness, and she shut her eyes tight.

'Put your head between your knees,' he commanded urgently.

She bent over, her hair parting around her neck. Her skin was creamy and vulnerable, but beneath the soft exterior, she had the courage of a goddess.

'Take a couple of deep breaths,' Andrew instructed, his heart pounding furiously. If she fainted, she could topple over the side.

'I can't come down to you,' he said again. 'That ledge won't hold my weight. You'll have to climb up.'

She glanced at him, then her gaze held steady.

'Imagine my arms around you, Stacia. Imagine I'm holding you, never letting you go.' The trust in her eyes made his heart tremble. 'Keep your back to the wall,' he added, 'and edge your way to a standing position. Look up, not down.'

She placed her hands flat against the wall, and slowly, surely, eased herself upright.

In his heart, Andrew cheered her on, not wanting to distract her by speaking aloud. Maria's boat passed directly in front of them, seemingly to mock them as it bobbed gently up and down in the water.

'Keep your eyes on me.' He spoke loudly this time to cover the sound of the boat's engine, and was relieved when it disappeared from view around the outjutting rocks.

Stacia's face filled with determination and she did as he suggested.

'Now lift your hands to mine.'

She twisted her head as she looked up, her cheek against the dirt as she examined the cliff's surface. Then she pressed her hands harder, as though her fingers were all she had to keep her glued to the cliff face.

'I can't do it,' she said at last, her skin a pasty white.

'You have to,' he said fiercely.

Her eyes filled with worry. 'I can't let you help me,' she said. 'Your wound . . . it's bleeding.'

'That's not important.'

'It is to me.'

'I'm fine.' He stared steadily down at her, willing her to do as he said.

Slowly, ever so slowly, she edged her hands skyward, and he leaned farther over the cliff. He pressed as close to the ground as possible, his wound plastered against the dirt, and his blood reddening the earth beneath him. Pain sucked the air from his body. He thought he might pass out. Stacia's eyes were black with fear, but the courage she had drawn upon to face Andropolous was there also, all the more powerful because she possessed it despite her fear.

Andrew stretched a fraction further and his fingers met Stacia's. When they intertwined with hers, a current flowed between them, exchanging heart for heart, and with it their strength.

'Now turn,' he instructed softly, 'so you're facing the cliff.'

She caught her lip between her teeth.

He wished he could make it easy. 'Don't worry,' he said. 'I'll hold you.'

She kept her gaze skyward, didn't look at the danger below, and slowly, carefully, shuffled her way around. Pebbles and sand littered the ledge upon which she stood, and more skittered down as her body brushed the cliff. She blinked her eyes, no doubt blinded by the falling sand. But perhaps that was better. The less she saw, the less she'd be frightened.

With a swift release of hands, an un-crossing of arms, and a swifter re-grasping, Stacia stood positioned on her tip-toes, holding onto Andrew by his wrists. He clutched her wrists also, determined never to let her go.

'Now what?' she asked, a tremor in her voice.

'Now you climb,' he answered gently.

Her eyes widened.

He tightened his grip.

'Trust me,' he exhorted, his heart echoing in his ears. She smiled at him shakily, but her smile was filled with trust. With legs that seemed locked, she slowly, inexorably, raised her right foot. She edged it into a fissure and crawled a step upward.

He held onto her with his hands, and also with his eyes. If he could retain her gaze, he could get her up safely. He focussed past the pain in his bleeding wound and knotting shoulders, and concentrated instead on pulling her up a few inches.

He edged his body backward as she moved upward, anchoring them with his toes. The wound from the bullet bled more profusely then ever, but the courage and trust in Stacia's eyes lent him strength.

'You're almost there,' he whispered finally.

Her head topped the cliff. Dirt fell ominously around her as she scrabbled for a foothold in the freshly eroded soil. He braced himself on his elbows, and rose to his knees.

Stacia's grip on his wrist suddenly loosened, and her foothold fell away. He held on tightly as for one endless moment she hung in space.

She scrabbled for another foothold and Andrew got to his knees. Hanging half on and half off the cliff in a tug of war between life and death, Stacia managed, with one final pull from him, to fight her way up and over the edge.

He fell backward and she sprawled across him, both their strengths gone. Her breathing suddenly grew so slow and steady, he thought she might have fainted.

He sifted his fingers through the silky strands of her hair, and felt his heart swell knowing she was safe in his arms.

Stacia felt in Andrew's arms as though she'd come home. When he breathed, she did, too, felt grounded and safe by his body's presence. She crushed the fabric of his shirt between her fingers, and never wanted to let go of him again.

'You saved my life,' she whispered.

'You saved mine,' he answered.

'I almost got you killed,' she protested.

'If you hadn't cried out, Maria's man would have shot me.'

'Without me, you'd have your diamonds.'

'None of that matters.' His voice was heavy with fatigue and pain. 'As long as you're safe.'

'One is never safe,' she denied, knowing love held more danger than all else together.

'You're safe with me,' he insisted.

'I never asked to be.'

'Travel tip number four.' His smile was gentle. 'You don't always get what you ask for.'

A heat swept through her that was anything but safe, and Stacia slowly bent and kissed him. His lips were gritty with dust and salty with sweat, but they sparked in her a desire so intense her limbs shivered.

'I need you,' he said, his words vibrating against her lips. His groan of desire was like a whisper on a summer's night, and when his tongue met hers, her senses swirled.

She longed to revel in the passion, drown herself in it, but behind the sensuous release of feelings, she knew he was in pain. With a mighty effort, she pulled her lips from his.

'We have to do something about your wound.' Blood covered his chest and now her blouse. 'We have to get you to a doctor.'

'Later,' he said hoarsely, reaching one

arm behind her neck to pull her back to him.

'Now,' she said, holding firm against his hand. Unbuttoning his shirt, she examined the spot where the bullet had hit. Still impossible to tell if it was lodged in his body. The grim set to his jaw frightened her, as did the lines around his eyes. She gently stroked his cheek, wishing her touch had the magic to dispel his pain.

'We have to get that wound looked at,' she said, feeling helpless. 'In this heat, it could become infected.'

He ran his hand down her back. 'It won't,' he insisted.

She rolled off him and grasped the tattered hem of her blouse. With a hard yank, she'd ripped off enough cloth to bind his wound, and tied it carefully around his shoulder.

'Let's go,' she said, struggling to her feet. She held her hand out to him. His weight was more than she'd anticipated. Halfway to his feet, he pressed his palm to his shoulder. His skin paled beneath his tan and his breathing grew shallow. When he looked at her, his eyes were wide and dark.

'Can you make it?' she asked, gripping his arm.

With a nod, he staggered upright and pulled his hand across his eyes, blocking his pain from her view.

'Do you have a boat?' she asked. 'My boat left.'

He nodded again.

'Are you sure the fisherman waited?'

For an instant he looked confused, then his expression cleared. 'I came on my own,' he said. 'I wondered how you got here ahead of me.'

'How did you convince a fisherman to let you take his boat?'

'Wasn't easy,' he said. 'Must have trusted me, I guess.' He shot her a shaky grin. 'Money helped.'

'How far is your boat? Can you make it?'

'Yes,' he said.

Admiration swelled within her. He would do what needed doing by sheer guts and obstinacy. 'I'll help you,' she said, praying he would let her, praying, too, that she was strong enough to hold his weight. She released his hand and moved to his side, ducked in under his arm and stood tall to support him.

He made a sound as if to protest, then a smile flickered across his lips and he gave her shoulder an assenting squeeze.

Warmed, Stacia led the way along the cliff to the trail she had climbed before. It seemed so long ago now, yet every rock, every blade of grass, every inch of the path was embedded in her mind. She glanced down and shuddered, knowing the descent would be worse than climbing up.

Andrew leaned heavily on her. If she slipped on a patch of gravel, they would both fall. Jack and Jill tumbling down the hill . . .

Andrew's color had worsened and his lips were pinched white at the corners. Despite the bandage she had applied, he was bleeding profusely, and as his blood drained, so would his strength. It was excruciating to listen to the shallow rasping of air from between his lips.

She stared again at the path, and caught her lower lip between her teeth. Easier to look down than to see the pain on Andrew's face. As though connected to him by an invisible cord, every stabbing agony he endured transmitted itself to her.

She took a firmer grip on his waist and concentrated on the ground immediately beneath her feet. She tried to ignore the slithery twists of the path beyond.

The sun was higher now, and hotter, as it reflected off the sea and shafted blindingly upward. Her body soon dripped with sweat, the drops running down her skin in dusty rivers. Andrew's skin was dry, as though a fever burned through him, sucking away his fluids.

He needed a doctor. And soon.

She risked another glance at the trail. They were about half way. Five minutes more and they'd be at the bottom.

Andrew's boat was beached on the gravel shoreline. She had only to push it into the water, climb in, start the engine, and aim it in the right direction. All things being equal, she'd have no problems at all.

Yet for all the sweat flooding her skin, the inside of Stacia's mouth was dry with worry. A sense of urgency claimed her. She tightened her sweat-slick fingers around Andrew's waist and stepped resolutely over a fissure in the path.

'We're almost at the bottom,' she said encouragingly, not liking to see the blood ooze from between his fingers as he held his hand over his wound.

'Good,' was all he said.

Thirty feet. Twenty. Ten. Suddenly, they were there. The stones on the beach crunched beneath their feet.

From the top of the cliff, the boat had seemed the easy part. Stacia stared at it now with dismay. She'd been in a motor boat once with her father, both of them encased in over-large life jackets.

She remembered her father pulling the starter cord, and only a sputter had emerged from the engine.

Andrew dragged his arm from her shoulder and before she guessed what he intended, tried to shift the boat further into the water.

'Stop!' she shouted, grabbing him by the arm. She slipped between him and the skiff. 'I'll do it,' she said, glaring at him.

'You're not strong enough.' His face was grim.

She ignored him, grabbed hold of the bow, and heaved on it mightily, but the boat didn't budge. The gravel crunched behind her.

'You will not touch this boat,' she ordered Andrew, refusing to even look at him, concentrating instead on the task at hand. She strained harder and managed to rock the boat until it's stern floated higher in the water. Amazingly, when she tilted it back again, the rest of the craft slipped like a fish into the sea. Stacia pulled it around so its stern was to the beach.

'Well done,' Andrew said.

Stacia's cheeks filled with heat. She held the boat steady, while he half-climbed and half-fell into its hollow middle, then he crawled toward the bow, his face white and strained.

Stacia gave the skiff a push and stepped into the water after it. The cool liquid lapped at her ankles first, then went up over her knees, feeling wonderful after the heat and dirt of the cliff climb.

She scrambled over the boat's side, and crouched low to balance, as she'd seen her father do that summer so long ago. The boat's keel scraped bottom.

'Push off with an oar,' Andrew suggested. He sat slumped against the craft's aluminum side, his legs stretched between her feet.

There were two oars in the bottom of the boat. Stacia tugged one out, found it heavy and unwieldy. Cautiously, she stood and thrust it into the water, pushing off against the bottom as she would with a pole. The boat slid away from the shore and Stacia plopped down hard onto the metal seat.

Andrew closed his eyes, but whether to keep off the glare of the sun or to conceal his pain, Stacia wasn't sure. She swiftly dropped the engine into position, then searched desperately for the knob the marina attendant had shown her father.

There. She found it. She pulled out the choke and caught the starter cord between two fingers, murmured a swift prayer, and tugged as hard as she could. The engine caught with an ear-shattering roar. She slowly pushed in the choke, and the roar gentled.

13

Stacia laid her hand on Andrew's knee, and was comforted by even that brief contact. She kept her gaze on his face, not wanting to watch as the doctor swabbed away the blood from the place the bullet had hit.

Andrew was looking like Ulysses again, an injured warrior lying on his shield. But Andrew was real, a flesh and blood hero who was all her own.

'You were lucky,' the doctor said to him, as he straightened and reached for a jar of antibiotic powder. 'Falling over a cliff could have killed you, but landing on a sharp stick . . . ' The elderly doctor clucked his tongue.

Andrew had insisted they lie about what had happened, guessing rightly that the bullet had only grazed his shoulder and passed on by without lodging in it. He said the Greek police were jumpy enough since the airport explosion. If they told the truth about stolen diamonds and villains with guns, they might both end up in jail in place of Maria Argolis. Stacia hated the lying, but knew they had no choice.

'Will he be all right?' she asked, watching as the doctor shook antibiotic powder into Andrew's wound, then covered it with a bandage.

'A good night's sleep, no exertion for a few days and he should be fine,' the doctor cheerfully reassured her. He taped down the last end of snowy cotton, gave Andrew his hand and pulled him to a sitting position. 'He'll be uncomfortable though. Come in tomorrow and I'll change the dressing. We don't want any infection.'

★ ★ ★

Stacia stared down at Andrew, worry twisting her belly. His face was flushed and sweat beaded his brow. Was his wound infected or had she simply piled on too many blankets?

His eyelids flickered open. 'Stop frowning,' he said, 'and come lie next to me.'

She took hold of his hand and gave his fingers a gentle squeeze. 'You need sleep,' she said firmly. He'd been restless since returning from the doctor's office, despite the pain killer the doctor had prescribed.

'I need *you*,' he insisted. He took his hand from hers and ran his fingers up her arm.

Stacia's pulse began to race. She needed him too. A chilling thought swept through her, killing the desire. Andrew could have died. So could she.

He tugged on her arm and lifted the corner of his blanket, motioning to the place beside him.

She remained where she was on the edge of the bed. 'You have to sleep,' she said sternly.

'I will,' he promised solemnly.

Stacia drew her bare feet up onto the bed and slipped beneath the covers. She felt shy, all at once, of his nearness and heat and of choices made in the cold light of day.

'I want to hold you,' Andrew whispered. 'Crawl over to my other side.'

She swung her leg over carefully, not wanting to touch anywhere near his wound. Her breath caught when his manhood pressed against her, but she rolled swiftly to his other side. No matter how much she wanted to make love with Andrew, they couldn't do it now, not with him hurt.

She could tell by the rapid rise and fall at the base of his temple that Andrew's pulse raced as swiftly as her own. His breathing had quickened also, matching hers, then speeding past. He rolled onto his uninjured side and faced her, his wound high and uncrushed.

'You have to sleep,' she said again, trying to say the words as though she meant them, and trying not to want him so.

'I am sleeping,' he said, nuzzling her ear. 'And having the nicest dream.'

'I'll leave unless you behave. I'm not going to be responsible for your injury getting worse.'

His lips twitched. 'I'll be good.' He adjusted his features to those of an angel. 'But can you?'

A devil, not an angel.

She turned away and put her back to him, but her awareness of his body stretching against her didn't abate. Her bones felt soft, her nerve endings alert, her will to resist non-existent. A single gesture and she would turn to him without question.

'Good night,' he whispered, holding her close.

She longed to turn and kiss him, but didn't dare start what they couldn't finish. Instead she forced her eyes shut and took a deep cleansing breath. If she could still her mind, could erase the magic of their previous lovemaking, then perhaps she could sleep.

His breathing was soft, its rhythm soporific. Finally, at last, her own breathing slowed. Her muscles unbunched, and a languorous calm engulfed her, beguiling her toward sleep.

★　★　★

Warm skin, slow hands, hard body pressing hers.

With a sigh, Stacia buried her nose into her pillow, trying to keep hold of the pleasure-filled dream.

Firm lips tracing a path across her shoulders . . .

Her eyelids snapped open, and awareness flooded over her as clearly as the morning sun shafted the bed. 'Andrew,' she said softly.

'Stacia,' he murmured back, nibbling her ear.

'You'll hurt — '

'Shhh.' He kissed her neck. 'I'm fine.'

'How can you be fine?' Although his lips felt fine.

'All better.'

'You're not — '

'All better might be an exaggeration, but feeling damned good.' He stroked the bare skin below her panties.

'The doctor — '

' — said rest. I know!' He urged her over on to her back. 'But I've done enough of that.'

'But — '

'No buts.' He captured her lips with his, and kissed her with such a thoroughness, she was left breathless. 'I've been waiting all night to make love to you.'

Andrew gathered her into his arms and rolled on to his back, pulling Stacia on top. It was as though a banked fire had sprung to life, the instant heat intoxicating. She captured him with every sense; her taste tingling his tongue and her hair falling about his face, engulfing him in the perfume of flowers. The pain in his shoulder dulled in the exhilaration of her presence.

Her body melted into his and heat built within heat. He explored the hills and valleys of her curves, breathed in her scent and drowned in her essence.

This was no apparition haunting him with her memory, but a flesh and blood woman, alive and safe in his arms.

He hadn't failed her as he had failed his wife Nancy.

Slowly, cherishingly, he ran his hands up her back. Her skin was warm and pliant beneath his fingers. She buried her face into his neck and kissed him, every spot her lips touched becoming electric with desire.

He delighted in the satiny softness of her skin and her delicate beauty. Cupping her face in his hands, Andrew was struck to the heart by her vulnerability and strength. He wanted to explore every part of her body, to know her so intimately they would be as one.

His thumb ran along her jaw, then upward over her cheekbones, brushing back her hair, its weight shimmering against his fingers. The early morning sun splashed their bed, catching her fully on the face. Trust shone from her eyes and tugged at his heart, before her lashes lowered and concealed all expression.

Andrew eased away the hindrance of her blouse, his desire quickening as his hands stroked her naked flesh. Womanly curves met his touch, with womanly dips and hollows. He unhooked her bra to release her breasts, took a nipple into his mouth and caressed its nub with his tongue. With a moan, she pressed closer and moved above him.

He needed her, wanted her; her skin and her breasts, as well as the moist folds between her legs. He cupped the curve of her buttocks and pressed her closer, her warmth penetrating through the panties she wore. She lifted her hips and he eased her panties off.

One moment her breasts were close enough to kiss, the next out of reach while she kissed him. Her tongue was hot and moist, fanning his flame.

When she drew near his bandaged shoulder, her kisses slowed, and she looked at him, her eyes filled with sympathy. Capturing her lips, he kissed her worry away, feather kisses to heal, hot kisses to arouse.

With a smile, she moved lower, her hair a perfumed waterfall as she trailed kisses along his chest. Within and without, his heat flamed to fever pitch, then she pulled off his undershorts and the fever became an inferno.

The goddess that was Stacia slid damply along his chest, her skin silkily, burningly sensuous. Scarcely able to breathe, he slipped his hands along her thighs, and brought her legs forward, his manhood reaching for and finding her. She pressed against him as he entered, urging him to drive.

But he moved slowly. Her pelvic muscles squeezed, released, then squeezed again, trapping them both in a rhythm beyond control. Soft sounds escaped her lips, and she arched upward, her eyelids dropping over her expressive eyes.

Overwhelmed by her heat, he thrust upward once more. Her lips parted and her breathing grew shallow, while a sheen of perspiration appeared on her skin. Slowly . . . sensually, she opened her eyes and stared in wonder down at him, as her body joined with his on a roller-coaster ride to the stars. In an ecstasy of sensation, they moved together to the magical moment of release.

Tears dropped from Stacia's cheeks and hit his chest, mingled with his sweat and christened their love. With a final convulsive shudder, her body stilled, and her breathing deepened to a slower rhythm.

Andrew held her close, wishing they could remain like this forever, suspended in the giving and taking of pleasure, able to laugh and love and forget the world and its danger. But it wasn't possible to forget. With a sigh, he kissed her hair in a final caress.

Stacia had never felt so alive, so strong, so beautiful, so perfectly content. Then she smiled into Andrew's eyes, and her happiness died.

'What's the matter?' she whispered, propping herself up, then rolling off him as though they had never touched. The lost contact with his warmth chilled her to the bone.

'We have to leave,' Andrew replied. He winced as he swung his legs off the bed and with effort managed to tug on his pants.

'Leave?' she asked, not able to hide her disbelief.

Andrew turned to her, his eyes clear and very blue. 'I'll go to the travel agent. You pack.'

'Pack? Where are we going?'

His lips tightened. 'We were shot at yesterday.'

'I know.' She glanced at his bandage. 'That bullet was intended for me.'

'Which is why I'm booking a flight to Athens,' he said grimly.

Relief washed over her. They were going to Athens. Away from Crete. Away from Maria Argolis.

'I'll give you some money for a hotel there — '

'Money? Me?' Her head began to spin. 'What about you?'

He picked up his shirt from the floor. 'I'll join you in a day or two.'

'Where will you be until then?' She pulled her legs loose from the covers.

'Tying up loose ends.'

'There are no loose ends. Maria Argolis has your diamonds, but she got away. That's the end of it.'

Instead of answering, he chose an orange from a bowl on the dresser. 'Eat this,' he said, tossing it to her.

She flung it back at him, refusing to be side-tracked.

'No telling when your next meal might be,' he told her lightly, though his taut shoulders denied the lightness of his words.

'What do you intend to do?' she persisted.

He shrugged, didn't answer.

Realization and fear pressed in together, turning her skin clammy. 'You're going after Maria,' she whispered.

He pulled his shirt over his head and struggled through the neck opening.

She grabbed hold of his wrist. 'If *you're* going, *I'm* coming too.'

'Not this time,' he said, his eyes deadly serious. 'You're going to Athens. This doesn't concern you.'

'Of course it concerns me. I brought

those diamonds into Greece. I'm going to help you get them back.'

'This isn't just about the diamonds.'

'What then?'

'You were almost killed.'

She felt suddenly breathless. Perhaps now he would say the words of love he hadn't yet spoken. She was ready now to hear them and say them in return.

'I was afraid — ' he began.

Her heart soared. These were not words of love, but she could tell that he cared.

'I wish to hell you hadn't been on that island. We'd made our plan,' he growled, 'and that wasn't it.'

Her heart stopped in mid-flight, plummeted straight back to earth.

'I couldn't let you go alone,' she protested. 'When I thought that's what you'd done, I had to follow.'

'Which is why you're going to do exactly as I say now.' Andrew stared at her with determined eyes. 'I need to know you are safe. I want you to go to Athens.'

'No,' she said fiercely. Her fingers formed

fists. She would never be safe if the man she loved was in danger. 'I won't go without you,' she added quietly, 'especially as it's my fault Maria's got the diamonds.'

'If you had been hurt, it would have been *my* fault.' He gripped her shoulders. 'Maria Argolis and her gang are deadly serious. I have one death on my hands already. I won't have another.' He let go of her suddenly and Stacia jerked backward.

'It was your wife who died,' she said numbly, wondering why it had taken her so long to figure that out. Perspiration formed between her shoulder blades and slid damply down her back.

'Yes,' Andrew answered.

'What was her name?' she asked softly.

'Nancy,' he replied.

'How did she die?' Stacia asked, bracing herself for the answer.

Andrew's eyes went blank, as though he were looking inward, then he shuddered and re-focussed on Stacia's face. 'Maria Argolis did it,' he said, his expression turning to stone. 'I knew there had to be someone else, that the fellow the police caught was too stupid to pull off such a theft on his own. But I didn't know who killed Nancy until I heard Maria talking in the fortress.'

All sound had died except for the thumping of Stacia's heart, and it filled her ears until she heard nothing else. Heat pricked her body. Every nerve-ending pulled taut.

Andrew passed a hand over his brow, then as though his strength had left him, sat abruptly on the bed. Stacia touched his knee, but if he felt the pressure of her fingers, he gave no indication.

'When?' she whispered, not taking away her hand. He needed her even though he made no sign.

'Eight years ago.'

'A long time.'

'Not long enough.'

Stacia's chest tightened. He obviously loved Nancy as much now as he had when she was alive. 'How?' she asked. Maybe talking about it would give him some release, would dispel the demons eating his soul.

'I had begun the Brokerage the year before,' Andrew answered, 'worked night and day to make ends meet. I cut corners, cut costs, but bought only the best gems.' He stared down at Stacia's hand, didn't look into her eyes. 'People began to notice my work, began to trust my word, knew if they asked for a particular stone, I'd either have it or could get it for them.'

'It became a point of pride to deliver what people wanted. I went abroad for my gems to Africa, India, and Australia.' A yoke of sweat turned the neckline of his tee-shirt damp.

'And your wife?' Stacia asked, a chasm opening in her heart, the love inside disappearing from sight.

Pain savaged Andrew's eyes. 'Her father was one of my best customers. I supplied the diamonds for the necklace he gave her on her twenty-first birthday. Went to the party to watch him present it to her . . .'

And fell in love, Stacia realized numbly. She stared at the sunlight shimmering in through the window, not wanting to hear how much he loved another woman.

'We got married two months later.'

She glanced back at Andrew, found his face ashen.

'A year after that, she was dead.'

Dead, but still loved. Stacia's heart ceased its wild racing, leaving nothing behind but a hollow echo where the pounding had been. A silence descended, the swish of the ceiling fan the only audible sound.

It was revenge Andrew was after, as well as the diamonds. Revenge for his wife and the love he had lost.

Stacia felt as though her heart had been flung into a void. She would never be alive in the same way again. Would never laugh, never love, never lay her head on Andrew's chest and know when she was with him, what it was like to be home.

'It was my fault she died,' Andrew

continued, the pain in his voice penetrating her despair.

'How?' she asked again.

'I left her alone too much, for weeks at a time sometimes.'

'You were building your business. You had to do what you did.'

'That's what I told myself. I pretended it was for us, for our future together, for our children and a secure home. I didn't admit the reality to anyone.'

'What reality?'

His eyes were black pits. 'That I loved what I was doing, loved the adventure and danger, the wheeling and dealing, the high-flying life. And Nancy let me do it. She let me pretend.' His shoulders sagged. 'Because she loved me.'

'Her death wasn't your fault.'

'I was at a client's home when Maria and Kosta Argolis broke into our house.' Lines scored Andrew's forehead, added age to his face. 'My office at that time was in our home. I kept everything there. Stupidly thought it was safe.' He swallowed hard and stared at his hands. 'When I came home, I found her dead.'

Stacia took his hand in hers, found it icy cold.

'Maria got away unseen. Kosta was captured. A neighbor had seen him leave and gave a good description to the police. They soon picked him up. But catching him didn't save Nancy.' His eyes filled with rage. 'Only I could have done that and I wasn't there.'

Nothing she could say would make any difference. Nothing she could do would erase his guilt. No matter how much she loved him, he couldn't love her back. All she could do was stroke his hand, and that was as much to comfort herself as it was to comfort him.

'So you're going to Athens,' Andrew finished, slowly extricating his fingers from hers. The tenuous link between them broke with the movement.

Sorrow filled Stacia, for Andrew and

his wife, but also for herself and her broken dreams.

She'd been right about love. It didn't keep you safe. She wrapped her arms around her chest, cold beyond shivering.

14

She should be upstairs packing. If she was going to leave, she should just go, not wait for Andrew to come back from the travel agent with her ticket. He intended she go by plane this time, wanted her off this island as quickly as he could remove her. Wanted her out of his life.

She should want that, too. Stacia stared at the postcards in the rack in front of her, unable to keep her brain from playing back everything Andrew had said, everything he had done, how he had touched her, kissed her . . .

Fool! She riffled the cards impatiently, their pictures blurring from the tears in her eyes. It didn't help remembering how Andrew's lips had scorched her breasts, or feeling, still, his hardness inside her, full where she had been empty, joyous where she had been sad.

Her heart ached with remembering.

She pulled a postcard from the rack, then put it back again unread. She touched her elbow and her fingers trembled. It was the last place Andrew had touched her. She could still feel his heat.

They had walked down to the lobby together, but he had left her there, cold and bereft, with money to pay their bill and instructions to pack her things. She couldn't go to Athens and leave Andrew to face the danger alone.

She shut her eyes. Despite the lobby's dim light, her pulse hammered relentlessly against her temples. A dull ache crawled up her back and the cuts on her legs burned. She felt like crying, but crying wouldn't make Andrew love her.

The realization hit her in a blinding flash. Whether Andrew loved her or not, she wasn't going to Athens. She straightened her shoulders. Andrew might not love her, but she loved him, and she was not going to Athens until she was sure he was safe.

Her mind made up, Stacia glanced toward the reception desk. The hotel owner's nephew appeared to be asleep. His chin nodded to his chest and a faint snore bubbled through his lips with the regularity of a ticking clock. The owner would be upset if he walked in now, as he had been yesterday when the maid, another relative, failed to bring his tea on time. Happily, the young girl had handled her uncle with the aplomb of a diplomat.

That same maid had been tidying Stacia's room the day before when she and Andrew had returned from Spinalonga Island. She had chatted to them with the vivacity of youth, spilling her family's secrets as airily as shaking out the blankets. Stacia bit her lip. She felt at home here, comfortable. Another reason she didn't want to go.

She would simply remind Andrew she was on vacation, and that she intended to see something of Crete before she left. She'd find a quiet cafe and write some postcards. Nothing dangerous about that. One to Angela, one to her friends at the library, one to old Mrs. Franklin who lived next door. And when Andrew had finished his search for his diamonds and Maria Argolis, when he came back unsuccessful, but safe and sound, that's when she'd leave.

Feeling slightly happier, Stacia reached out and chose another card. A quick glance, then another, then she peered at it more closely. The stone church on its front looked familiar. She was sure it was one she had seen before. Old stone, old style, a plain church for a devout people, a structure to stand the test of time, trouble and war.

She moved closer to the window, and held the card up to the light. She *had* seen this church before, and that twisted tree beside it, its trunk gnarled and bent from the force of the wind. It was the church in the picture on Mr. Stone's desk — *Wilson's* desk, according to Andrew. There had been a woman in that picture. A Greek woman standing next to a Greek church.

Maria Argolis, the woman Stacia had known first as Mary Argyle. No wonder she had seemed familiar. It hadn't been her resemblance to Grandmother Roberts at all. Thank heavens for that. It didn't seem nice, somehow, comparing her grandmother to a killer.

Maria and Wilson, Wilson and Maria. Together. A team. Maria had been younger in the picture, as Wilson had been younger. Her hair had been black, and Wilson, now bald, had a full head of hair.

Stacia turned the postcard over. Eighteenth century church in Artemis, Crete, the card said.

Her mouth went dry. She now knew where Maria Argolis must have gone. Running back to her own village like a fox to its lair, believing herself safe there, never guessing anyone would look.

A street map of Agios Nikolaos was pinned to the far wall, and next to it stretched a map of the island. Stacia moved toward the map, dizzying excitement racing through her. She forced herself to move slowly, was grateful when, gradually, a steadying calm descended.

Artemis was difficult to find amongst the hundreds of villages dotting the island, but at last she spotted it at the end of a long secondary road. It was situated in the middle of the mountain range that ran like a dragon's spine down the length of the island.

From a pocket below the map, Stacia extracted a folded tourist pamphlet. A map of the island was printed in bold black and white on the inside, the actual roads designated in various shades of grey depending on their quality. The road to Artemis was so faint, it was barely visible.

But there would be a bus to the village. Buses left Agios Nikolaos at every hour of the night and day. If Andrew needed his diamonds back, wanted revenge, they could get both by hopping on a bus.

★   ★   ★

Andrew held on to the travel agent's door for a second, so that when it closed it would close gently. He would like nothing better than to slam it shut, but until he found Maria Argolis, he'd hang on to his temper.

At least he had Stacia's ticket. Although getting it had taken far longer than he'd expected. The clerk had mumbled something about tourist season and over-booking while the line-up in the office grew. It wasn't until Andrew threatened to charter a plane from a competitor that the clerk found a seat, miraculously for this very afternoon.

Now to get Stacia on it, which given how she felt about leaving, promised to be more difficult than threatening a corporation.

When he'd told her to get packed, her mouth had tightened in mutiny. Packing, at least, shouldn't take her very long. He'd seen how she'd stuffed her clothes into her suitcase at the Chicago airport. Andrew glanced at his watch. Three o'clock already. The plane left at six. Lengthening his stride he hurried toward the hotel.

He came at it from the rear, dodging between the tables of the open air restaurants at the edge of the canal and casting a swift glance upward toward the fourth floor.

Stacia's balcony doors were closed. No clothes clung wetly to her railing, no half-finished drink sat on the metal table outside. Andrew heaved a sigh of relief. With any luck she'd have finished her packing, paid their bill with the money he had given her and was hopefully sitting in the hotel lobby awaiting his return. She might even have packed his things as he had given her a key to his room.

He'd get Andreas to meet her in Athens. No, not Andreas. His partner in past business dealings was too interested in women. He could be trusted with diamonds, but not with Stacia.

It would have to be Stavros, who wouldn't enjoy acting as guard dog. But he would do it if asked, for the man was more a good friend than an employee, had been with him on the day he found Nancy dead. Stavros would understand he had to keep Stacia safe.

Andrew walked around to the front of the building, and was momentarily blinded by the afternoon sun. He stepped off the narrow sidewalk to let a woman and her baby carriage pass, then hurried the few remaining yards to the hotel entrance.

He paused in the doorway to give his eyes time to adjust to the gloom of the lobby, then he glanced around the room. There were no bags at the reception desk, and no sign of Stacia.

Must be still packing. He strode toward the stairs. Faster to walk up than to wait for the ancient elevator to creak its way down. Besides, he had to keep moving, was in no mood to stand still, couldn't bear to count the separate dings as the elevator passed each floor and know precious seconds were ticking by while he did nothing.

As he climbed, a sharp ache hammered

his temples and his wound hurt more than he liked to admit. Despite his discomfort, he took the stairs two at a time, was sucking in air by the time he pushed open the fourth floor door. Had to get back to his running. Hadn't done any on this trip. Although maybe it wasn't a lack of fitness that caused him to lose his breath, but the apprehension invading his body at the thought of losing Stacia.

A friend had once told him to visualize what he wanted, had insisted that with enough concentration, everything he desired would come true. Andrew grinned as an image flashed of Stacia walking out of the sea naked, her brown hair falling in a stream down her back. He forced the image out of his mind. He didn't have time for fantasy now, didn't care if it worked. All he wanted was to see Stacia perched on the edge of her bed, with her suitcases next to her, packed and ready to go.

He knocked.

No answer. No soft voice suggested

he enter. No quiet movement. Nothing. The pounding in his head grew fiercer. Andrew put out his hand and turned the knob.

Unlocked.

His breathing stopped. The memory swept over him of Nancy lying on the floor, dead in a pool of her own blood. His lips tightened, his hand lifted, and he turned the door handle, hoping he would never see such a thing again.

Stacia's clothes were still heaped across heaters and chairs. Her suitcase sat untouched on the floor of her closet. Her bathing suit still hung from the bathroom door, and her camera was perched on her bedside table. Even the book she'd been reading the day before had its book mark still placed neatly inside. Apparently no bent pages or broken spines were permissible for a librarian.

The only thing missing was Stacia.

Andrew whirled around and headed back down the hall. As he descended the staircase, a man and woman drew aside to let him pass, a young couple walking with their arms around each other, their faces flushed from the sun or the heat of their own passions. Andrew swallowed hard.

If anything happened to Stacia . . .

This time he let the door slam as he passed through it. The desk clerk jumped to his feet from a semi-doze.

'Room 412,' Andrew demanded. 'Miss Roberts. Have you seen her?'

The young man's brow furrowed.

Andrew longed to shake him.

'I saw her earlier,' the spotted youth said, his lank hair flopping over one eye. 'She went out.'

'What do you mean *out?*' Andrew leaned across the desk. 'Out where?'

'Said something about Artemis.'

Andrew's self-control scattered and he grabbed the front of the clerk's cotton shirt.

'She . . . she wanted directions to the bus,' the youth stammered hastily. 'Said to tell you to wait for her.'

Silently counting to ten, Andrew

forced his fingers to release him. 'What's Artemis?' he demanded.

'A small village in the mountains.' The youth pointed toward the far wall. 'It's on the map.'

The village was a mere pin-prick compared to Agios Nikolaos, which was itself not very big. Andrew turned back to the clerk. 'What else did she say?'

The boy shrugged. 'I told her if she wanted woven rugs there were better places to visit than Artemis.'

'She wants woven rugs?'

'Why else would she go to the mountains?' The youth came out from behind his desk, picked up a smoldering cigarette butt from the dirt around a potted plant, and flicked it out the door.

Andrew's stomach lurched. Stacia couldn't go anywhere. Not with any safety. Then the hotel door flew open and suddenly she was there.

'Andrew,' Stacia cried, unprepared for the thrill racing through her at the sight of him. 'Thank goodness, you're back.'

'Where have you been? You've got to

get packed. Your flight leaves in a couple of hours.'

'Forget the flight,' she said impatiently. 'I know where Maria Argolis is.' She watched his face, wanted to see in him the excitement she already felt.

'What do you mean, you know?'

'She's in Artemis, a small village in the mountains.'

'How the hell would you know that.'

She held up the postcard she'd found on the rack. 'When I picked up the package at Wilson's house, I saw this same church, with Wilson and Maria standing in front of it, in a picture on Wilson's desk.'

'That doesn't mean a thing.'

His expression hadn't changed at all, hadn't taken on the excitement she had been anticipating.

'It means she's been there,' Stacia insisted, 'probably is from there.'

'That's a big jump, Stacia.'

'It's a place to start!'

He shook his head. 'It's far more likely she's left the island altogether, gone to Cyprus, Turkey, perhaps.'

'Then why do you want to search for her here?'

'I have to make sure, have to pick up their trail.'

'Well, I know she's in Artemis.' Stacia suddenly felt more certain than ever.

'Woman's intuition?' he asked skeptically.

'She said she had a safe place to hide on Crete,' Stacia reminded him icily. 'I've been to the bus station, checked out the schedules — '

'This doesn't change anything, Stacia.'

'Of course it does.' She grabbed his arm, wanting to shake him. 'We know where she is now.'

'I've got your ticket to Athens and I want you on that plane.'

'There's no way I'm going to Athens. Not now.'

'Nothing has changed,' he repeated. 'Not as far as you're concerned.'

'I found out where Maria is.' Stacia's cheeks blazed with heat. 'You're not going there without me.'

'Who says I'm going there at all.'

'Of course you're going.'

'I'm not.'

'I don't believe you,' she cried. 'This is the best lead you have. You won't just ignore it.' She stood as tall as she was able. 'And I have to go too. If it weren't for me, you wouldn't even know *where* to look.'

'If it weren't for you, a lot of things would be different.'

Guilt swept back, hot and heavy and disheartening. 'I know,' she admitted, wishing for the millionth time she had found some way to keep Andrew's diamonds out of Maria's hands. 'That's why I have to help.'

Andrew turned toward the reception desk. 'Ring a taxi,' he barked at the now wide-awake clerk, then without another glance in Stacia's direction, stormed up the stairs.

He could think again if he thought she was going to follow. Fury burned Stacia's face. Within five minutes, Andrew was back, her suitcase gripped in his hand. He grabbed hold of her arm and pulled her out the door. The taxi he ordered was already waiting by the curb.

'Get in,' he said, yanking open the taxi's door. 'Airport,' he instructed the driver, once she was safely inside. He thrust an airplane ticket in through the open window.

'Aren't you coming with me?' she demanded hotly. 'At the very least to make sure I get on the plane.'

'You'll be on it,' he said. The expression in his eyes told her she had better be, then he slammed the door behind her and slapped the taxi's roof.

Stacia leaned forward, too furious to look back. 'To the bus station,' she told the driver, feeling inside her pocket for some of the money she had borrowed from Andrew days ago.

★ ★ ★

The hot vinyl caught damply at Stacia's thighs as she slid across the seat and

319

peered through the fly-specked window. Far more people than seemed possible to fit on one bus stuffed their luggage into the compartment along the bus's side or threw it to the driver waiting on the roof. There couldn't possibly be seats for everyone, but no one seemed to care. It was as though this were a party and they were all invited.

She had left her luggage with the taxi driver, instructing him to take it back to the hotel and give it to the desk clerk. She didn't want to be encumbered with anything that would slow her down. What she needed now was speed.

The bus schedule indicated that tonight at eleven, a bus would return to Agios Nikolaos from Artemis, giving her plenty of time to get up to Maria's village, prove Andrew wrong, and get back again tonight.

Maria would be there. Stacia was sure of that.

Andrew would be furious, and in all likelihood would be there, too, for she was sure he had lied in order to get rid of her. Stacia frowned. If he had lied, why wasn't he on the bus? Perhaps he was intending to rent a car, which, unlike her, he could afford.

Stacia wiggled in her seat, and rolled her shoulders, tried to shake off the sadness weighing her down. She had left alone and in a fury, was still angry with Andrew, but most of all she wished that things could be different; that Andrew's business was not at risk because of the diamonds she'd smuggled and lost, and that Andrew was in love with her, not with a woman who was dead.

The bus filled rapidly with elderly men and women carrying bright scarves knotted into bundles; middle-aged women, whose handsome faces shone serenely despite the confusion, and middle-aged men with rounded bellies, plump faces and sharp black eyes.

The younger people's clothes were peacock bright against the black attire of their elders. Although not many young people traveled by bus, preferring no doubt the small scooters Stacia had seen careening around town, or the over-burdened and under-powered trucks that chugged along the highway.

But even without the young, more people came, the line twisting down the steps, out the door, and along the pavement.

One young woman, with flashing eyes and jaunty hips, sashayed down the aisle. Her lipstick matched the scarlet blouse showing so vividly beneath her sweater. There were baubles on its front, reminding Stacia of the sweater she had given to Maria.

The young woman had two little girls in tow, twins by the looks of them, and a baby in her arms. She seemed too young to be the mother of three, as she flounced into the seat in front of Stacia and settled the children around her. The baby's sudden wail overcame the girls' chatter.

An old woman followed the four down the aisle, and as she passed the young woman, plucked the baby from her arms. She clucked soothingly to the child as she sat down in the seat next to Stacia.

The baby stared at Stacia, tears glistening on his cheeks, then another torrent of sound emerged from his O-shaped mouth.

Stacia gazed at him helplessly. The twin girls swivelled around and stared with wide eyes over the chair back. The young woman paid no attention, stared out the window instead, hunching her shoulders against the sound.

Stacia thrust her hand into her multi-colored tote bag and prayed the souvenir she had bought on the ferry to Crete for her friend Angela's new baby was still in her bag.

Something hard met her fingers. She pulled out the gaily painted wooden minotaur, and held it toward the baby. The child's howls died midscream, and he lurched toward the mythological monster in a straight-backed lunge, nearly tumbling off the old woman's lap.

Hastily, Stacia handed him the toy.

The twin girls stared at their brother, then at each other, then they giggled behind their hands. The young mother turned around and smiled gratefully at Stacia. The old woman grinned tooth-lessly.

'My sister's boy,' the young woman said, pointing toward the baby.

'Not yours?' Stacia asked.

'No,' the woman said, looking horri-fied at the notion. 'Sister sick. My mother took children. Sister wants them back.' She rolled her eyes as though she thought this incomprehensible, yet she gave her nearest niece an affectionate pat.

The old woman nodded and smiled. She obviously didn't understand the words but was enjoying the interaction between her loved ones and this foreigner. She jabbed her bony finger into her own chest and said, 'Sophia.' Then she pointed to her daughter in the seat ahead and proudly said, 'Natolie.'

'Stacia,' Stacia said slowly, pointing to herself.

Sophia was totally unlike Stacia's

own grandmother. The old woman appeared much softer. Although, perhaps they weren't so different. After Stacia's mother had died, Grandmother Roberts had stepped in as this woman had done, and had tried to instill in her grand-daughter what she knew to be right and wrong.

Which was probably why Stacia was in this pickle. If she hadn't listened so well to what Grandmother Roberts taught her, she wouldn't have cared enough about anyone else to want to help them. She would have looked out for Number One.

★ ★ ★

Andrew glared at the road in front and pressed furiously on the gas pedal. Still the car failed to increase its speed. The car rental man had nodded vigorously when questioned about the car's capabilities, had said it was the fastest they had and would suit an American, had even added a verbal *vroom, vroom,* as though the sound effect would indicate how fast was fast.

Not very fast as far as Andrew could make out. But they'd had nothing else and he'd been anxious to get going.

With a frustrated sigh, he pulled the car up in front of the hotel. Five minutes to collect his bag and he'd be off. No telling where he'd be going next after he checked out Artemis. He hadn't admitted it to Stacia, not wanting her to become even more insistent on accompanying him, but his instincts told him Maria Argolis probably was in Artemis or at the very least had gone there first after leaving Spinalonga. If she was there, he'd find her.

He drew his room key from his pocket, and pushed open the hotel door. He saw the luggage before he moved another inch.

Familiar luggage. Suitcases he had carried in both Greece and Chicago. Suitcases that shouldn't be here at all. If Stacia's luggage was here, where the hell was she?

★   ★   ★

Stacia shut her eyes, and prayed the wooziness would go away. Probably wouldn't abate until the bus finally stopped, or the corkscrew twists in the gravel road straightened themselves out. As long as it wasn't some cursed traveler's stomach. She didn't think it could be the food, for she'd eaten nothing since last night. She was probably just hungry, should have listened to Andrew about the orange.

With a shudder, she pried open one eye and squinted out her window. It was dry here in the mountains, the ground rocky and the grass spiky. Yet goats munched contentedly along the side of the road, clinging to the rocks as they'd been born to do, with the only sign of their owners being the faint whisper of smoke from far off chimneys.

Perhaps they had no owners, were simply pets of the Gods. The landscape was ethereal enough to imagine Zeus himself looking down from on high and raising his arm in some godly decree. She hoped he would intervene if the bus went off the road.

There seemed little holding the road to the mountain except a few olive trees, their leaves shimmering even without a wind. One misstep, one false turn of the wheel, and they'd all plunge to their deaths. Stacia fought the bile crowding her throat.

Yesterday's cliff hung in her memory. Only this time there was no Andrew to offer her his hand, to hold her eyes with his strength. This time her sole protection was a casing of thin metal and a driver who drove like a crazy person.

The bus rumbled around another turn, its gears grinding in protest, and the ground dropped alarmingly away as the bus seemed to balance on three wheels. Sharp knuckles prodded Stacia's arm, forcing her gaze from the window.

Sophia peered at Stacia anxiously, her weathered brow furrowed into a thousand wrinkles. She held out her hand. Pumpkin seeds lay in her rounded palm, a few spilling out each time the bus swayed around a curve. The woman picked them off her dress and carefully placed them back in her hand, then offered them to Stacia, her face creasing into a smile.

Stacia's stomach quailed at the sight of food, but she forced herself to reach for the seeds. Perhaps if she ate, this sick feeling would disappear. If she were going to look for Maria Argolis, she had to be strong.

Sophia's smile widened, and she murmured something to another elderly woman across the aisle. This woman peered around Sophia at Stacia, then rummaged in a bag at her feet. Eventually, she pulled out a rounded loaf of bread and a piece of waxed paper, from which wafted the pungent smell of *feta*. She solemnly passed the food to Sophia, who placed it straight into Stacia's hands.

She shook her head in protest, her

stomach still rebelling, but with smiles and a vigorous waving of her hands, the woman across the aisle insisted. It seemed all the passengers were watching, as though national pride was at stake that she eat the food offered. Smiling weakly, Stacia tore off a crust of bread, laid a sliver of *feta* on top, then brought the bread to her lips.

Her stomach seemed to calm as soon as she swallowed. Ambrosia of the Gods couldn't have tasted better. Even the jerking of the bus as it ran over a rock had no negative impact. Swiftly, she ate more. The little girls in front clapped their hands and giggled, and Stacia grinned back at them, rubbing her stomach to show how much she had enjoyed the food.

'Olives?' Natolie asked, thrusting a jar at Stacia.

'Thank you,' Stacia replied, plucking out a plump one and popping it into her mouth. She couldn't believe how much better she felt, how mere food could make such a difference.

Although it wasn't just the food. It was the women and the fact they cared. Moisture pricked Stacia's eyes as she smiled at the friendly faces. Andrew might not be here, but she wasn't alone.

15

The sun was still hot as Stacia descended from the bus, but when she ran her hand up her arm, her skin felt icy. The impulse to turn back was overwhelming, to endure anything rather than look for Maria Argolis, even if it meant riding on a bus where the driver kissed the good luck charm hanging from his mirror before recklessly passing other vehicles in oncoming traffic.

Artemis was smaller than Stacia had imagined. A single shop and two or three houses straggled untidily along the road. Beyond that, there was nothing. She wasn't sure what she had expected, but she had imagined at the very least a cafe, some place she could catch her breath and gather her courage.

And where was the church?

Behind her, the driver revved the bus's engine, then with a strident blare of his horn, swung the vehicle out onto the road. She took a step after it, but stopped as the bus roared down the road away from her, gravel and dust churned up by its wheels.

A hand touched her elbow. 'Sta..cia,' Natolie said, pronouncing the foreign name haltingly, 'you have friends meeting you?'

'No,' Stacia said. If only she had. She took a second glance around, praying that by some miracle a proper village might appear. 'I . . . I'm looking for someone.'

Natolie translated what Stacia said to Sophia, while shifting her nephew to her other arm. She gestured impatiently to her nieces to stop playing in the dirt.

'Come,' she finally said, signalling Stacia to follow her and her family. She led the way to a rocky path leading up the hill. 'I bring you to my mother's friend. Sometimes she takes in guests.' She gave Stacia a swift smile. 'She take in you.'

'I won't be in Artemis long,' Stacia

said. Just long enough to find Maria and prove Andrew wrong. 'I'm catching the bus back to Agios Nikolaos tonight.' She'd tell Andrew where Maria was and, together, they'd retrieve the diamonds. Perhaps then, the guilt she felt would disappear.

'Who you want to meet?' Natolie asked, her brow furrowing with the effort of speaking in English.

Stacia thought for a moment, not certain how much she wanted to say. 'A woman,' she finally replied. 'Maria Argolis.'

The old woman, Sophia, spat in the dirt, and muttered under her breath.

'Do you know her?' Stacia asked.

Natolie flushed. 'My mother no likes this Argolis.' Her brow wrinkled further, and she gave a helpless shrug. 'Maria Argolis is bad woman. Bad family.'

Excitement shot through Stacia, followed swiftly by fear. Maria Argolis *was* known to the villagers. She had begun to worry that Artemis wasn't the place to look, that because there was no church, there would be no Maria Argolis. She didn't want to fail, didn't want to return to Agios Nikolaos without finding the woman.

'Where does Miss Argolis live?' she asked.

'Beyond the village.'

'This way?' Stacia asked, glancing up the path they were climbing.

'Yes, yes,' the young woman said impatiently, 'but further, beyond the village.'

'Isn't that the village?' Stacia asked, gesturing back the way they had come. The shops were smaller from this height and almost hidden from view by a few small shrubs.

Natolie laughed, and said something to Sophia. The old woman cackled and herded the children faster.

'The village is ahead,' Natolie said, a grin still flashing on her face. 'Bus not always goes through town. Only on market days.' She shrugged. 'Too much trouble for bus to go up steep hill.'

A hilltop hideaway. Perfect for Maria.

'Road to town,' the young woman

continued, pointing to her right, 'is over there. This trail is — ' She chewed her lip. ' — short-cut.'

Even as she said the words, they topped the crest of the hill. Stacia stopped walking. Ahead of them was the church, as well as the tree. Just like in the postcard, and in the picture on Wilson's desk.

Stacia's young friend tugged her elbow and she moved forward again, toward the village and toward the church. Her face must be white for there seemed no heat left in her body, but she mustn't show fear, for if she stopped herself from showing it, perhaps the fear would disappear. In any other circumstances, she'd have been charmed by the building's beautiful grey walls, and by the lushness of the trailing vine working its way up the stone. Incredible to see such lushness in the midst of such dryness, and the ancient graveyard on the hillside beyond had its own unique beauty. Each grave was tended, each graveside shrine filled with the pictures and possessions of the one who had passed away.

The poets of ancient Greece would have appreciated the scene, would have composed songs in its honor. But to Stacia, a horror overshadowed the beauty, and with stiff, awkward movements, she followed Natolie and her family past the church Maria had stood beside and on into the village.

Sophia's friend's house was small and poor, yet her two room abode held such comforting warmth and brightness, it forced Maria Argolis and the evil she represented to recede from her thoughts. It wasn't until Maria's name emerged in the stream of Greek flowing between Natolie and her grandmother's friend, that Stacia's fear flooded back.

'Auntie Helena says Maria Argolis is bad woman,' Natolie whispered, glancing worriedly at Stacia at this confirmation of her grandmother's opinion.

'Is she in Artemis now?' Stacia asked.

'Yes,' Natolie said. Her frown deepened. 'Auntie say Argolis family helped enemy during the war.'

The expression on Natolie's face told

Stacia this was the worst of all possible damnings.

'I have to see her,' Stacia insisted, trying to force away the fear invading her limbs. 'Where does she live?'

'Beyond the church,' Natolie answered reluctantly. 'Up behind the graveyard.'

Stacia peered from the doorway into the encroaching darkness.

'I come with you,' Natolie offered.

'No,' Stacia refused. Despite her longing to accept the younger woman's offer, she couldn't willingly draw anyone else into the nightmare.

Natolie took off her sweater and placed the black wool garment around Stacia's shoulders. 'It's cold,' she explained, with troubled eyes.

'Thank you,' Stacia said solemnly. She placed her arms through the sweater's sleeves and pulled it tight around her, then she walked towards the church swiftly, not daring to glance back.

At the church, Stacia could see the roadway leading to the Argolis house, but she averted her gaze, peered into the church instead. Following a sudden impulse, she stepped inside.

It seemed smaller than it had appeared outside, and shabbier, too, though not from lack of love and attention. The prayer books in the pews were frayed with age, and only stubs of candles lay in the box next to the statue of the Blessed Mary, but fresh flowers sat beneath the altar, and a crisp lace cloth with exquisite embroidery lay on the table holding the statue.

The figure of Mary, with its promise of serenity and safety, drew Stacia's attention, but when she reached the statue, she saw its eyes gaped sightlessly. The colored glass which should have depicted them had been broken or lost over the years.

Stacia slowly stretched out her hand and touched the hollow where the glass should be. Despite the statue's disarray, a calm stole over Stacia, and penetrated the misery in her heart. She had lost her mother, her father, and now Andrew, too, but Mary's sightless eyes told her what her own eyes had failed to see, that she loved them all and that to love took courage. Whether Andrew loved her back or not, she had to do whatever she could to help him.

A sense of her own strength filled Stacia's heart and gave her the courage to leave the church. Darkness now smothered the day, and a mist had descended, whispering wetly against her face. With grim determination, she started up the roadway to Maria's house. She kept to the shadows of the trees lining the road, glad of the darkness, not wanting to be seen.

Too soon, she arrived. Maria's house was a two-story block of grey plaster blending into the silver of the olive trees beyond. No vehicle stood in the driveway and no sound came from within.

Stacia crept closer, pressing flat against the house, the plaster knobby beneath her fingers. She cast a swift glance into the narrow basement window to her right, but a wooden box against the glass on the inside blocked her view.

She had to *see* Maria to know for certain she was in the village. Until then, she had nothing to report back to Andrew. Perhaps around the back there'd be something to indicate occupancy. She tiptoed softly, but her feet still crunched the gravel, and her breath seemed, all at once, to be coming in too swiftly.

A glance around the back garden revealed nothing but blackness, so slowly, warily, she approached the back door. She turned the door handle and found herself in the kitchen where the smell of cooking hung heavy in the air. Crockery sat on the table, and roast lamb congealed in fat lay nauseatingly on the plates.

Two plates, Stacia counted. There was still just the two of them. Maria and her stupid, yet strong, helper. Two against one. Four against one if you counted their guns.

One against nothing if no one was about.

With that thought, a plan presented itself that was better than the one she had conceived in anger. A plan not involving heroics or the smashing down of doors or even worse, the waving of guns. Maria might not be here, but Andrew's diamonds perhaps were.

A quick in and out would be long enough to find the diamonds, then she would run as fast as her legs could carry her back to the village and the nearest phone. It had worked for the purse snatchers at the Athens airport. They had got away. So could she.

Stacia ducked beneath a braid of garlic, and edged past the table towards a door on the opposite wall. Beyond was a narrow hallway, lit only with the light filtering through from the kitchen. There were two doors off the hall to the left and three to the right. Stacia stared at them, willing them to give up their secrets. Finding Andrew's diamonds might well be as chancy as choosing the right door on a television game show.

A wooden table stood next to the front door at the far end of the hall, and above the table hung a cross. Incongruous to see a cross in the home of a killer.

Stacia tiptoed down the hall and opened the far door on her left. A sitting room much like Grandmother Roberts' room had been — empty, cold, and neat.

She retreated and worked back along the right side of the hall, sparing the bathroom a cursory glance before moving on to the study.

It was a small, dark room, with no window to allow in the light. Papers were scattered over the desk, maps mostly, with the Mediterranean's tiny coves marked in red X's, and routes drawn from one island coastline to the next. Meaningless rows of figures and letters were scrawled down the map's sides, but nowhere in the room was the black sweater with Andrew's diamonds.

Disheartened, Stacia returned to the hall. Before she could take another step, a sound emerged from the door opposite, a door which must lead to the basement below. With the sound terror came sweeping into her breast.

'Shift those crates closer to the stairs,'

Maria's voice barked.

Instinctively, Stacia backed away, moving as far as possible from the door blocking her from Maria. In her movement, a board creaked beneath Stacia's foot. Her hand flew to her throat which contained her snagged breath.

'Not there, you fool,' came Maria's voice again, irritated now, angry. 'Over there so I can get by.'

By great good luck, they hadn't heard her. Not sure she still breathed, Stacia moved rapidly down the hall and tried to open the front door handle. Locked. No exit that way.

Footsteps sounded on the basement stairs.

Frantic now, Stacia yanked open the door to the right and found herself staring up a dark stairwell. She hesitated, terrified to go up to the second story, sure that if she did, she'd become trapped there like a cat up a tree.

The footsteps echoed louder.

'Andrew,' Stacia murmured, using his name like a talisman, hoping the pulse now drumming against her temples would cease, as would the perspiration running in rivulets between her breasts.

Stacia reached for a barely discernable railing, expecting to find the warm smoothness of wood. Instead, she found the cool chill of metal. It took everything she had to keep her fingers in place and raise her foot to the first step.

After that, it was easier. The instinct to put as much distance as possible between Maria Argolis and herself forced her onward. She blindly felt her way, tried to listen for other sounds, and focus her attention away from the pounding of her own heart.

As she climbed, she counted the steps. Only twelve, but there seemed more. The upstairs hall when she reached it was like the one below: long, narrow, and dark, with more black rooms to each side.

From below there now came no sound at all.

The room opposite the stairwell had an open door, the master bedroom from all appearances. A chill swept Stacia's body, for suddenly she knew. If the sweater was anywhere in the house, it would be here in Maria's bedroom, the place every woman kept what was important.

She listened again for the sound of footsteps. Again, she heard none. She tried to gauge if she had time to look for the diamonds and if she did, would she have the courage to attempt it. Clenching her fists, she slipped across the hall.

The faint odor of lilac hung in the bedroom. Stacia's stomach lurched. It had been the lilac perfume which had first drawn her to Maria, the lilac which had reminded her of Stacia's own grandmother. The scent now spelled danger.

She stood motionless and let her eyes grow accustomed to the room's deeper darkness. A muted light came in at the window, a reflection, perhaps, from the village below, where other people sat safe in their houses, talking and laughing with the people they loved.

Loved. She could almost feel Andrew's hand on her shoulder, the warmth of his fingers, the strength of his soul. She pushed away her longing and felt her way towards the bed, not daring to turn on the overhead light lest its glow shine through to the grass outside.

The bed was unmade, its covers flung back and pillow dented. A suitcase lay at its foot with a pile of clothes heaped beside it. But it was the bedside table which drew Stacia's gaze, for on it lay the sweater. She took it up, its soft folds of wool warming her hands.

A broad sweep of light suddenly illuminated the room, causing shadows to dance against the far wall. Stacia ducked to the floor, her heart pounding against the sweater she held crushed to her chest.

She crawled to the window and peered out into the night. A truck had arrived, and was now backing toward the front door. Stacia crept back into the hall, and crouched there, listening. She heard the front door open, and her skin turned to ice.

'Maria,' a man shouted. 'Are you ready?'

This surging of blood and numbness of limbs must be how it felt to have a heart attack. The more intently Stacia listened, the faster her heart beat.

'You took your time,' Maria answered, her voice increasing in volume as her feet echoed along the downstairs' hall.

Heavy boots thumped towards Maria's voice. Adrenaline surged through Stacia. She had to get out, but there seemed no escape. Muffled footsteps now sounded behind a door at the far end of the hall. A back staircase, which, like the front one, connected the two floors.

No time to think, no time to plan. Stacia darted across the hall and down the front stairs, not caring now whether or not anyone heard her. She flung open the door at the bottom and saw that the hall was empty. For an instant, relief swept through her. Then she tried the front door, and her relief turned to panic. Whoever had come through had re-locked the door behind them.

'Who's there?' Maria shouted, her voice a frozen shard that pierced the ceiling separating them.

Stacia ran towards the kitchen, but saw through its open door a man standing with his back to her peering into the garden. She plunged down the stairway leading to the basement, hopefully a place filled with nooks and crannies into which a person could squeeze. Instead, she found a white-washed box of a room with a single bulb illuminating its surface. Wooden crates were piled high along the walls.

She twisted, turned, then twisted again, but there was no place to hide.

The footsteps pounded closer.

★ ★ ★

Andrew slammed on the brakes and for the umpteenth time cursed the mountain road. God alone knew how Stacia's bus had made it around these bends. With one hand on the horn and the other on a crucifix, no doubt, that seemed to be the way things worked here on Crete.

It was getting dark. Andrew's fingers tightened around the steering wheel. He had to find Stacia, had to keep her safe. This wasn't a game where the shots fired were blanks. He took the next curve faster than the last.

★ ★ ★

Maria Argolis walked slowly down the basement steps, one hand on the railing, the other on her gun. A gun whose barrel was trained on the center of Stacia's forehead.

Stacia pressed flat against one of the wooden cartons. Her stomach knotted. If she was *Alice in Wonderland*, the boards would reform to make a barrier. But this was no fantasy where safety came on demand. She stared into Maria Argolis's eyes. This was real.

'You should have left well enough alone, my dear,' Maria said, her voice softly menacing.

Stacia stood as still as she was able, afraid to move, or even to breathe, lest the gun erupt as it had before.

'And where's Mr. Moore?' Maria asked, her voice scratching the nerves along Stacia's spine.

She shrugged in response, not trusting herself to speak.

'Is he here?' Maria demanded.

'No.' Thank God, he wasn't. No matter how much she longed for the comfort of Andrew's arms, she couldn't bear to see him hurt.

The satisfaction in Maria's eyes almost hid the shadows on her face, the signs of stress in her voice, and the lack of sleep. She laughed at Stacia's answer, but the laughter was hard and grating.

'It's better this way,' Maria said. 'He'll suffer more alive than dead. As he did the last time, when his wife was killed.' Her eyes glittered with malice. 'Did he tell you about that?'

'Yes,' Stacia whispered.

'He thought it was my brother who

killed her. My brother, who's still rotting in jail because of Andrew Moore. *My brother.*' Maria screamed the last words, as if her brother were the important one, not the woman he had killed. She seemed half mad in the glaring light of the uncovered bulb, for her eyes burned in the icy whiteness of her face.

Maria pointed to the hard cement beneath Stacia's feet. 'Pick up the sweater,' she commanded.

Stacia bent at the waist, her body so stiff with fear, she almost couldn't bend at all. Her fingers were stiff, too, and when she grasped the black sweater, she found her arm shook.

Remaining where she was, Maria gestured curtly to her helper, who had appeared on the stairs behind her. He descended the steps two at a time and snatched the sweater from Stacia's hand. As he did so, his gaze roved insolently over her body.

'Take her upstairs,' Maria directed. She grabbed the sweater her helper threw. 'Lock her in my study, then get back down here and load the weapons into the truck.'

'Weapons?' Stacia repeated.

'In the crates behind you.' Maria's smile was reptilian.

The crates Stacia had imagined might help save her. Full of weapons. Her head swirled.

'The best weapons money can buy,' Maria gloated. 'Or should I say diamonds.'

The dizziness extended to Stacia's limbs, causing her to sway as though she were at sea.

'You use diamonds to buy weapons?' she asked. Andrew's diamonds?

'Saves selling them when they're hot. Diamonds for weapons, weapons for money.'

'But who are the weapons for?'

'I don't ask,' Maria snapped. 'It doesn't pay to be too inquisitive in this part of the world. You should have learned that by now.' Her face took on a knowing expression. 'But that bombing in Athens . . . '

'Was a bomb you supplied?' Stacia's stomach churned as she remembered the fear on fellow passengers' faces.

Maria shrugged.

'Three people were killed.' Stacia didn't even attempt to keep the horror from her voice, a horror seeping into the marrow of her bones.

'As long as I'm paid, what does it matter? They can blow each other to kingdom come for all I care.'

Andrew would care. She cared. Stacia pressed her eyes shut. If she could call to mind Andrew's touch and warmth, perhaps it would help, would make her feel less alone. But it was impossible to dispel the images the weapons conjured up, of shooting, and bombs exploding, of people dying.

'Why not shoot her here?' Maria's helper growled. 'Why take her upstairs?'

Maria turned her flinty gaze on him. 'Do as I say,' she snapped.

The man's fingers bit cruelly into Stacia's arm, and he jerked her toward the stairs. As he dragged her past

354

Maria, she felt the evil emanating from the woman and every nerve in her body screamed in protest.

On the top step she stumbled and fell to her knees, jarring her leg against the door sill. The man jerked her up again, and yanked her along the hall, taking as little care as he would with a sack of potatoes. Once in the study, he shoved her into a chair and bound her hands and feet.

There was no question of a struggle. Not with Maria following behind, her gun trained on Stacia's back, and death in her eyes. She squeezed past Stacia's chair, something new in her hand now.

'A bomb,' Maria said, carefully holding the object up. She smiled again, even more coldly than before. Slowly, carefully, she placed the bomb on the desk. 'Just like the one in Athens. This one's set to go off in forty-five minutes. Once I press this timer, it'll tick away the minutes until it blows up, taking you with it.'

'Why are you doing this?' Stacia

whispered, her tongue thick and use-less.

'You know too much,' Maria replied coldly. 'Seen too much; our operation, our base, everything. Made it so we can't use this place again.' She glared at Stacia. 'You should have stayed in Agios Nikolaos, my dear. Shouldn't have meddled.' She frowned down at the bomb. 'I just wish Andrew Moore had come here with you. Then everyone who knows would be silenced.' She smiled a cunning smile. 'Never mind. We'll find him, and before we kill him, we'll tell him what happened to you.'

The thundering of blood through Stacia's brain couldn't shut out Maria's words. She had tried to make things better for Andrew, had succeeded only in making them worse.

Maria's hand inched forward and shifted the bomb so that its face was toward Stacia. So she could count off the minutes of her life, Stacia supposed. Could know to the second how much time she had left.

Maria's helper backed out the door as though he wanted to run, his gaze locked on Maria's hand as though he didn't trust it would take forty-five minutes for the bomb to explode.

Stacia wanted to run as well. Wanted to flee as fast as she could back to Agios Nikolaos and back to Andrew. She would never see him again now. Pressing her eyes shut, she tried to shake away her tears. Couldn't allow Maria to see her fear, or her sorrow, either. That would only make it worse, would give the other woman too much satisfaction.

'Well!' came a reedy voice from the direction of the doorway. 'I didn't expect to see you here, Miss Roberts.'

Stacia jerked open her eyes. 'Mr. Stone,' she said hoarsely. The bald spot on Stone's head shone as he bowed politely.

'Stone?' Maria inquired sharply. Her forefinger hovered above the bomb's ignition button.

'Just a little joke, my dear,' Wilson

explained. 'Diamonds. Stones.' He gave a depreciating shrug. 'It amused me at the time.' He turned back to Stacia. 'I'm sorry you ended up this way. But you shouldn't have angered my wife.'

Maria. His wife?

Wilson moved his head from side to side. 'No, really you shouldn't have.'

'Enough of this chatter.' Maria pointed a bony finger down the hall. 'Go help Niko with the crates.'

Her husband didn't move. Only his gaze shifted, as did Stacia's, to the object poised beneath Maria's hand. 'You should wait, my dear, until we're finished loading. No sense taking any chances. We want to be well away before that thing explodes, and once you've pressed the button, it'll blow up if you change the setting.'

Stacia hadn't been aware her breathing had ceased, but, suddenly, she gulped in air. Her chest heaved and twisted, as the terror locked inside struggled to escape.

Maria stared at her husband, her eyes

two burning fires, then she lifted her hand from the button and swept her hair back from her brow. She, too, seemed to be panting for air, but she moved away from the desk and out the door without another glance in Stacia's direction.

Wilson followed. Their footsteps echoed down the hall, taking on a hollow sound as they descended to the basement. The study door was partially shut, so though Stacia couldn't see, she could still hear. With grunts, groans, and sharp instructions from Maria, the two men heaved the crates up the stairs. They carried them down the hall past the study, and loaded them into the truck.

Leaving Stacia locked in what had become a nightmare. No matter how much she struggled, the knots in the rope refused to loosen. No matter how much she twisted and turned, she saw nothing in her line of vision that could possibly help.

Desperate ideas for escape whirled in

her head, but nothing could get past the numbing realization that she would never see Andrew again. Never hear the exhilaration of his laugh, or exult in the boundless energy of his mind, feel the tenderness of his smile, or the passion of his body.

In too short a time, Wilson and Niko had shifted every crate to the truck. Maria re-appeared in the study doorway, her eyes glittering with malice. She didn't pause, didn't speak, simply walked over to the bomb and re-set the timer's hands to read fifteen minutes. Then, with a swift almost reverent movement, she pushed the button.

'Still time enough for you to think,' she murmured, before crossing in front of Stacia and pulling the door closed behind her. With a harsh, grating sound, a key turned in the lock and Maria's footsteps receded rapidly down the hall.

The clock face might be visible from where Stacia sat, but the only sound she heard, muffled as though she were under water, was the slam of the front door and the growl of the truck's engine as it pulled out of the drive.

She sat as still as she was able. Only the nerve twitching beneath her right eye and her heart pounding its way through her chest let her know she was still alive. She nurtured a hope that if she didn't move, the hands on the clock would remain motionless also.

Then she heard it. A soft ticking. Inaudible almost, but as unstoppable as the drift of sand across a desert.

16

Metal squealed on metal as Andrew pressed his foot to the brakes, but they still worked, still stopped the car a hair's breadth from crashing through the stone wall of the church in Stacia's postcard.

He peered past the graveyard, straining to find the roadway the girl in the cafe had mentioned. She'd been standing in the restaurant's open doorway when he drove up, her gaze on the road in front of her, her face contorted into a frown.

Her eyes had lit with recognition when he asked after Stacia. The American woman from the bus wasn't back yet, she had said, but had seemed relieved he was there, as though he had lifted a burden from her shoulders.

Andrew shifted the car into gear, and rolled slowly past the graveyard. It would be easier to drive if there were lights on this road, or, at the very least, if the moon would come out.

Despite the gloom, he spotted the turn to the left and started up the steep incline. He kept his eyes averted from the graveyard, not wanting to be reminded of death while thinking of Stacia.

A truck flew over the crest of the hill towards him. Its lights pierced the darkness as it bounced and bumped down the dirt road. Going too fast, Andrew thought, wrenching his steering wheel to the right. No call for such speed on a road such as this. Following some inner voice, Andrew pulled off into the trees, cutting his engine and dousing his headlights.

The truck roared past. In the front seat of the cab, three white, set faces stared straight ahead. Anger rolled up from Andrew's belly and exploded through his chest, heating him through, burning.

Maria Argolis was in that truck, as

was Wilson and that stupid hulk from the beach. They were getting away.

With his diamonds. With Stacia.

The fury in his throat erupted into a growl, then just as suddenly faded to a whisper. He hadn't seen Stacia in the truck. Unless she was in the back, perhaps she wasn't with them. An iciness froze his fever, and cold sweat chilled his brow. Had they killed her already?

Andrew twisted the car key and fired the engine to life. Then he yanked the steering wheel to the left, and began to follow the truck. At the very last moment, some other instinct intervened. He pulled the wheel to the right and spun his car up the road towards the Argolis house.

With arms turned numb, he maneuvered the vehicle up the steep path. He couldn't stop his mind from whirling, couldn't halt the sense of panic, of dread that he was too late to save Stacia.

Gravel skewed from beneath his tires as he braked too sharply in front of

Maria's house. The girl in the cafe had said it was the only one along the cemetery road. He jerked open the car door and somehow his legs carried him to the front door. It was locked, and Stacia was nowhere to be seen.

Moving faster now, he started around the house. He stumbled in the darkness. Windows passed in a blur. The back door was unlocked, the kitchen unnaturally bright.

He shouted Stacia's name, wanting only to speak it in the soft whispers of a lover. He bellowed its syllables, longing only to caress.

A shout echoed through the hall like a rock down a well. Stacia froze, and ceased her effort to escape. An effort that had succeeded only in rubbing her wrists bloody. Hope flowed upward from some secret storage place in her heart, then just as swiftly died. Maria and her gang must have come back, must have decided in the end to shoot her before blowing her to bits.

The shout sounded again. Without

properly hearing his words or seeing his face, she knew it was Andrew.

'Andrew!' she shouted back, her voice threatening to fail. He pounded down the hallway toward the study, his footsteps faster than Maria's, heavier too. Stacia glanced at the time left on the clock and the gladness in her heart died.

'Get out, Andrew!' she screamed. 'There's a bomb.'

'Are you all right?' he shouted back, rattling the door knob.

Now that you're here she longed to answer, but knew if he was to live, he had to leave.

'Are you hurt?' he demanded hoarsely.

'No,' she croaked. 'Just go, Andrew. There's no time.'

'I'm not going without you.' His voice was muffled as though his head were bent. A scratching sounded at the lock.

'Your diamonds — '

'Forget the diamonds.'

'Maria's getting away.'

'It doesn't matter.'

'It does. You said it did.' She struggled to hide the pain in her voice. 'Because of Nancy.'

She heard a thump, as though he had flung his body against the door, then heard the dull sound of a palm flattened over wood. She could imagine that same hand on her, his fingers rough and warm against her skin. Her belly tightened with longing, and her heart filled with despair.

'What about Nancy?' he demanded fiercely, ramming the door again. Its solid wood held.

Stacia stared at the clock and wished the bomb would explode. A quick death was preferable to hearing of Andrew's love for another woman, but she pressed her eyes shut, and gathered her courage.

'That's why you're here,' she said softly.

'I'm here because of you.' He kicked the door as he growled out the words.

He couldn't mean what he said. He had loved Nancy and she, him. As anybody would. Andrew's glance, the touch of his hand, the lilt of his laughter, his strength — all were irresistible.

Metal rasped against the lock. Andrew swore.

Stacia opened her eyes and focussed them on the door, on the solid panel of wood separating him from her. She longed to press her fingers against his forehead, caress away the lines she was sure were forming there, convince him somehow that everything was going to be all right.

Her gaze jerked to the clock with its swiftly fleeing seconds and her breath deserted her lungs.

'Go, Andrew,' she urged him again. 'There isn't enough time to get me out. Find Nancy's killers.'

The scraping grew louder, more determined.

Her heart seemed to be beating in time with the seconds. Tick tock, tick tock.

Go Andrew. Leave Andrew. Be safe, my love.

With a final scraping sound, the door

swung wide. Andrew's face was as white as his hair was black. She had never seen him look so fierce, or so determined. Not in the deserted fortress, or on the cliff . . . She snatched her gaze from his and glanced at the clock.

Two minutes. Not enough time. Not when she had every feature to memorize, every nuance of expression to know. It would take a life time for that. A life time she didn't have, and he couldn't give her.

'Go, Andrew,' she whispered, desperation sapping her voice. 'There's no time.'

He raced to the desk.

'Don't touch it,' she cried. 'It'll explode if you try to change anything once it's been activated.'

He altered his direction in midstride, and dropped to his knees beside her, throwing down the jack knife he'd used to pick the lock. For a few seconds he struggled with the knots at her ankles, thinking, no doubt, they'd be faster to untie than to cut.

With her hands tied behind her back, she couldn't touch him as she'd like, but she could smell the night air in his hair, and the musky odor of masculine sweat. She parted her lips to say the words that would send him to safety, but he glanced into her eyes and the words died in her throat.

Suddenly, unbelievably, her feet were free. Andrew moved behind her to work on her hands. A fierce longing to live swelled up within her, along with other longings his eyes had awakened. She had dreams she hadn't dared to dream, desires she hadn't dared admit. Pressing back the images, she forced her gaze to the clock.

One and a half minutes. No time to know anything, or say anything, either, to speak the words of love she longed for him to hear. The sound of a vehicle broke through her fear.

'They're back,' she cried hoarsely. She struggled to keep her hands from twisting in their bindings, knew that any movement would simply make the ropes tighter.

With an oath, Andrew reached for his jack knife. The sharp touch of metal tore at Stacia's skin, but in the space of a heartbeat, her bindings were gone. Andrew grabbed her hand, his fingers pressing tight over the cut on her wrist.

'Let's go,' he said, glancing at the clock, turning white at the paucity of seconds remaining.

He pushed through the doorway with her, shielding her with his body. Then the front door burst open and the enemy stormed through.

'Stop,' Maria shrieked, raising her gun.

Stacia didn't need the pressure of Andrew's hand on her waist to race toward the kitchen. She expected as she ran to hear the sharp report of the pistol, to feel the searing pain of the bullet.

CRACK!

The wood splintered next to Stacia's ear. She dove through the doorway, Andrew close behind. She was vaguely aware of the kitchen door swinging shut, of Maria's muffled curses and the sound of pounding feet. Andrew jerked open the back door and Stacia stumbled through ahead of him, one instant in a race for the trees, the next, flying through the air as the house exploded.

★　★　★

For a long moment, Stacia was conscious only of light, of a light within a light shining on her face.

A heaviness lay along her back. Andrew's heaviness. He was on top of her, his body so still she couldn't tell if he lived.

The light came again. 'All right, Miss?' a man asked.

She blinked against the glare of the flashlight probing her face, didn't speak because her tongue had thickened and was now glued to the top of her mouth. She managed to nod and the light left her eyes. At the same moment, Andrew stirred.

'Stacia,' he said desperately, 'are you all right?'

'Yes,' she whispered. The dread in her soul disappeared. Relief he was alive made her heart sing.

He touched her cheek, and sighed. Then he nuzzled her neck, warming her with his breath.

'Mister?' spoke the disembodied voice holding the flashlight. 'Are you all right?'

Andrew's muscles tightened against Stacia's back, then relaxed again as if he'd only just realized the man wasn't Maria, or Wilson, or Maria's helper. With a grunt, he rolled off Stacia and rose to his knees, took her hand in his and helped her sit up.

She stared past him to the house, feeling as if she floated above the ground, taking note of her reactions, but not allowing herself to feel.

'Don't look,' Andrew said, pulling her close. But nothing could obliterate the desolation before her.

Andrew's heart pounded beneath her

cheek. She reached for its rhythm and strength, and lay against him for a long moment. Until at last she pulled away and faced the shattered inferno that had been Maria's house.

Villagers, no doubt drawn by the explosion, had encircled the burning house as they would a Halloween bonfire. Their faces were solemn in the crackling night air.

'Maria, Wilson . . . they all must be dead,' Stacia said numbly.

'Yes,' Andrew replied. He put his arm around her shoulders, as though to lock in what warmth remained.

'With their own bomb,' she added. As deadly this time as it had been the last. Three dead for three dead, but that didn't make it fair.

'Yes,' Andrew said again.

'But you're safe,' she said, looking at him now. A tiny portion of heat returned to her body. She touched his face, touched his hair, felt she could never touch him enough. For no amount of touching would release the pain from her heart.

'We both are,' he replied, and gripped her shoulders tightly, as though he was afraid she would disappear again.

'Safe.' She smiled shakily. 'I thought I hated that word.'

'And now?'

'I'm not so sure.'

'I'll make you sure.' Fiercely, he captured her lips with his.

'Home,' she murmured, when at last he released her. His arms felt like home, a place where all the pain and sadness in the world could never touch her.

'Not such a bad thing.' He stared straight into her eyes.

'No,' Stacia agreed. With Andrew it would be wonderful. Then his lips met hers and her thoughts dissolved in a blaze of sensations.

'I love you,' he said, when he finally drew away. His eyes looked blacker than the sky above, but there was a light in them she'd hadn't seen before. It seemed to flicker for her alone.

Everything grew still. Her blood stopped in her veins, and her heart ceased to beat. She was vaguely aware of the fire crackling behind her, of people walking to and fro, casting long shadows from the brightness of the flames. But every fiber of Stacia's being was concentrated on Andrew and the words he had spoken. The most terrifying, wonderful words on earth.

'I love you,' he repeated, his voice like his body, strong, firm and sure. He smiled into her eyes, and his soul touched hers. 'Free to love you at last.'

'Free?'

His face grew solemn. 'Nancy died because of my business. I couldn't fix that or change it. But I had to make sure it would never happen again.'

It would have, if not for him.

'Nancy wouldn't want you to feel guilty,' Stacia said gently.

'I know,' he said, pulling Stacia snug against his chest. 'She would want what was best for me. And that is you. But I couldn't love again until I put her to rest. Justice, not revenge. That's why I had to keep you safe.'

'For her,' Stacia said haltingly, her doubts returning. 'Not for me.'

'That's what I thought at first.' He captured her gaze with his. 'Then I fell in love and knew it was for you. I tried to deny it, tried to tell myself I was only interested in your safety, nothing else, even tried to convince myself that if we made love, my lust for you would be satisfied.' He kissed her again and for a long moment nothing more was said.

'But it didn't work,' he finally whispered. His tongue drew a fire across her lips. 'Because I fell in love with you.' He put both arms around her and held her tight. 'Because I needed you — '

She sank into his embrace, and let all doubts die. She wanted only to savor the moment, cherish it and him.

' — and you need me.'

'I do need you,' she admitted softly. Her heart expanded with the truth of it. She smiled. 'I'm getting a taste for this adventurous life, you know.'

He swore under his breath.

'Getting good at it,' she teased, her smile widening to a grin.

He captured her mouth and kissed her words away. 'You are good,' he finally said, darting hungrily back to her lips between each word.

'If I agree to let you keep me safe — '

He frowned.

' — you have to agree to let me keep you safe.'

He nuzzled her neck and sighed. 'I'll agree to anything,' he said, 'except letting you get into this kind of danger again.'

'What about your diamonds?'

'To hell with my diamonds.'

She tried to pull away, but he held her tightly.

'You don't want them back?' she asked innocently.

'Stacia,' he said slowly, as though her mind had been addled by all she'd been through, 'the diamonds are gone. Blown to bits.'

'Maybe not,' she said, shaking her head slowly. She grinned at the look of surprise on his face.

378

'What do you mean?'

'I have them.'

He stared at her, stunned.

'Natolie lent me her sweater — '

'Who's Natolie?'

'A girl I met on the bus.'

'The girl I met in the cafe,' Andrew murmured.

'I was cold. She and her mother were kind. The sweater was black.' Her sentences emerged too short and incoherent. Must be delayed shock, Stacia decided.

Andrew stared at her not understanding.

'Natolie's sweater had baubles on it,' Stacia went on patiently. 'Nothing fancy, not as sparkly as diamonds, but if you didn't look too closely, they seemed real enough.'

A groove formed on his forehead.

'When I actually had to go looking for Maria, I almost didn't go on. I went into the church, the one I had seen in the picture on Wilson's desk.'

His face darkened at her mention of Wilson's name.

'There was a statue of Mary in the church. Beautiful, but so sad looking.' Stacia shivered. 'It had no eyes. Lost the jewels from them. In the war maybe.' Stacia smiled. 'But she still had her strength and she gave it to me.'

'You have your own strength,' Andrew said.

Stacia stared into his face, saw the love and admiration there, and a warmth filled her soul.

'Too much of it sometimes,' he added. He squeezed her tightly, as though even now he was afraid she might disappear. 'Finish your story,' he said, kissing her brow.

'In Maria's basement,' she went on, 'when there was no place to hide — '

Andrew's eyes grew black.

' — when Maria was almost there ... I switched sweaters.' Stacia smiled, totally satisfied with the surprise flashing across his face. 'I turned your sweater inside out so the diamonds were hidden, and put it on, then gave Maria, Natolie's sweater.' Stacia shrugged.

'She never noticed.'

'She noticed,' Andrew disagreed, his face turning sober. 'That must have been why she came back. Her own greed.' He shook his head. 'It killed her in the end.'

'They were smuggling weapons,' Stacia explained, a shiver skittering across her shoulders. 'They used diamonds to buy weapons.'

Andrew caught her to him and for a long moment simply held her. 'I know just what we should do,' he said, releasing her at last. His eyes glowed in the moonlight. He rose to his feet and held out his hand.

She was grateful for his touch as she followed him to his car, grateful, too, when the policeman stopped them that Andrew was the one to answer the questions. She felt sapped of strength. Leaning into Andrew, she borrowed some of his.

When at last they were free to go, she sank into the front seat of Andrew's car. Her heart was still too full, the horror too near, to say anything. Andrew steered carefully down the winding road toward the village and parked the car in front of the church. Stacia turned to him, surprised.

'Inside,' was all he said.

It felt different entering the church this time, as though Maria Argolis's evil spirit had already passed from the village. The interior of the church still looked shabby and worn, but there was a warmth and peace that hadn't been there before. The cold shadow of Stacia's ordeal began to disperse.

Andrew smiled down at her, as though he knew what she was feeling, then putting his arm around her waist, he led her to Mary.

'Take off the sweater,' he commanded softly.

Stacia looked at him, not understanding, not wanting to leave the comfort of his embrace.

'I'll keep you warm,' he promised, reading her mind as he had been doing since the day they met.

Heat touched her cheeks at the look

of love in his eyes, and she tugged off the sweater and turned it right side out. With a small smile, she handed it to Andrew.

He looked first at the diamonds, then at her, then he kissed her long and passionately, in front of the statue of Mary.

It was as if they had kissed before God himself. Joy filled Stacia's heart, and with it came peace, originating from the man and blessed by the Saint.

Finally, slowly, Andrew drew his lips from hers. He took the sweater he'd held crushed against Stacia's back, and plucked two diamonds from it. These he placed on the statue's outstretched hand.

'We'll give them to Mary for the villagers of Artemis. They were good to you, helped me find you.'

'The villagers hated the Argolis evil as much as us,' Stacia said.

It seemed so right. So perfect. Almost as perfect as Andrew.

'What about you?' Stacia asked,

wanting to make sure. 'Your diamonds are very valuable.'

'I have something much better.' Andrew stared steadily at her, the light in his eyes speaking his love. 'My jewel is you,' he said firmly. Then he kissed her again, a kiss filled with promises.

THE END